THE CRY OF DRY BONES

N.T. McQueen

Praise for
The Cry of Dry Bones

"The best fictions are not simply an escape from our world; rather, the best fictions are escape into our world. A vivid continuous dream that forces us to look into our own belief systems as we explore an imaginary world that, on the surface, appears so different from ours. N. T. McQueen accomplishes this in the tale of Tesfahun in his novel *The Cry of Dry Bones*. Curses, whispers, rumors, and mysteries riddle the world of McQueen's novel in ways that give birth to a desire for a new mythology. The novel is haunted by one central quest: What is life without sacrifice? The novel brims with insights into the idea of sacrifice, the notion of the tribal community, and heroism. A timely novel from another time."

Doug Rice, author of *Here Lies Memory: A Pittsburgh Novel*

"Delivering excellent detail to create an alluring environment, McQueen's coming-of-age myth is as compelling as it is creative...Readers of myth and fantasy will find familiar patterns, but McQueen breaks the mold by using his knowledge of tribal practices. As an outsider to the Omo Valley region, McQueen displays reverence as an outsider writing about traditional practices and the experience of colonization."

The BookLife Prize

"The writing flows as smoothly as Ethiopia's Omo River where the story is set, and there are many eye-catchingly vivid descriptions of nature as well as fiercely memorable scenes, from the opening hunt to the biblical final act."

Sam Krymalowski, author of *The Man Who Came To Rent*

"*The Cry of Dry Bones* is a thought-provoking novel in a class of its own."

Essien Asian, *Reader's Favorite*

"Overall, I am so impressed with this novel. It has everything – grand themes, a complicated protagonist, superb language, a plot that moves, excellent world-building and scene-making – that is necessary to describe a novel as great. *The Cry of Dry Bones* is great, and I think you will think so, too."

Elison, author of *The Evolution of Love*

"This is an exciting tale that keeps the reader hanging on, hoping with each turn of the page, each violent encounter, that there is some escape for this young warrior from the rough, violent road he is on, and from all the horrible acts and injustices he has encountered. And, the author does not let us down in the end. In this amazing tale, N.T. McQueen takes us on an incredible journey that you will not want to miss."

Mitchell Waldman, author of *Brothers, Fathers, and Other Strangers*

"*The Cry of Dry Bones* is a vivid portrait of a young boy's journey as he navigates his way through changes that transform his life."

Ellen Mason, author of *No Space for Love: A North Korean Defector Story of Survival and Love*

For the children of the river and the bush

PART I

A loose tooth will not rest until it is pulled out.

I

Talk of curses fluttered among the Akara's lips as they lived in the shadow of the river. Rumors of drought and famine and war passed from hut to hut. Some whispered of a *mingi* child hidden among them.

Only days from his ceremony, Tesfahun walked through tall golden grass behind The Great Warrior, arrows perched at ready bows but his mind remained back at the village.

To the right, the river flowed where the Crocodile Man's truce with the long creatures who ruled the waters failed to reach this far north. The two hunters kept watch for both man and animal. Tesfahun's grip burned. His fingers hot and moist against the bow. Kelile's faint steps gave no sound into the morning air and he followed his movements, step for step, pause for pause. The ostrich feather atop his father's head flickered in the breeze, a silhouette coveted by boy and men alike.

A thicket of leafless bush concealed them. In a labyrinth of organic shield, he could not see anything but kept faith in his father's guidance. Hunched like apes, the two slinked through dead thorns. The hunter passed unscathed while the Tesfahun's inexperience lay marked across the skin of his cheeks and torso. Despite the calls of the birds, the land kept still. Kelile watched the earth, sifting between stalks. He stopped and pointed to the earth without looking at his son. Tesfahun approached in a trail of flattened grass. Dark pellets piled among the blades. He looked to his father who pointed to the mound then rubbed his fingers together.

What?

Kelile cinched his lips and looked upon his boy. He pointed. Tesfahun looked at the pile, the corners of his mouth dropped and brow creased as he knelt, reaching for one of the black balls. The pellet collapsed, moist against his fingertips.

Kelile nodded then prowled forward. Tesfahun threw the remnants into the grass as he followed, wiping his hand about his waist. Watching his father, he placed his fingers to his nose but smelled nothing.

They traveled further north. He studied the scarred lines of his that ran up and down his father's back, white and dotted. His own body, free of paints and scars, felt naked in his father's wake and he gave credence to the hope of adorning himself should they return with a kill.

Clouds overhead lumbered in their movements like long dead mammoths grazing celestial grounds. Tesfahun watched them move, marveling at the illusory speed. A black figure waning ahead made him quicken his pace, darting and ducking through the bush faster, light steps for fear of snakes.

When he caught up, his father motioned a fist, his eyes unwavering from what lay ahead. He gestured his hand and the boy stepped forward. He followed the stiff finger between a thicket scant with leaf and berry. He looked and saw nothing but watched as if he did. Looking from the bottom up, he examined until the trunk of the bush quivered.

Now he saw.

A slender leg seemed illuminated to him now. He looked for guidance and his father handed him an arrow instead. Tesfahun's fingers felt the rough crooked wood. His hands trembled as he slid the arrow back, resting it upon his fisted hand, the other with a vice grip upon the drawn string. All creation held its breath, ever deferent of the ancient testament of survival. Be blood or take blood. A static crackling invisible, silent, through bark and blade, man and animal.

With unsteady aim, he waited. Father and son. A boy in a man's trade. The warmth of blood spread through his veins. He stepped forward and the crack of a dried stick thundered in the stillness. The animal bounded high and terrified and he could see the fear in its black eyes. Tesfahun gave a wobbled aim and released. The lone arrow sailed, rattling into a bush.

A bow's twang sounded from where his father stood. A shriek split the chaos. The noise of the fleeing animal cried through the silence, no longer bouncing but tumbling, barreling through thorns and branches. He placed both his dejected hands across his eyes. The bow fell to the ground and the pressure behind his eyes felt eminent. A bony hand rested upon his shoulder.

Tesfahun opened his eyes. His father's other hand pushed his bow toward him. He took the it and raised his eyes to his father. The brow rounded, a meek tilt of his lips. An embarrassed yet comforted smile spread on Tesfahun's face.

Come.

They marched on, a paternal hand about Tesfahun's shoulders. They found the wayward arrow far from the kill, point first into the dry earth. Nearby, the deep hoof marks of the animal's escape could be seen, vibrant dark, blotches trailed into the brush now broken and disheveled by death's coming.

Did you hit it?

Kelile smiled a white smile.

Tesfahun's eyes grew wide, swelling with a sense of wonderment.

How?

Kelile shook his head. You have much to learn.

They followed the trail of blood, a crooked line of a broken path newly made. The heat arrived, hot upon their skin but with a soft breeze that cooled their bodies. Tesfahun turned every corner expectant, ready to see the motionless carcass.

It ran for a while.

The arrow pierced her belly. That is why the blood trail is so long. Longer than I thought it could run.

It must be strong.

He nodded. An honorable animal to be sacrificed to us.

They emerged from the web-like foliage to a flatland of grass and a fingerful of trees cast shade straight at their roots. Kelile surveyed right to left with a hand at his brow, bow slung on his shoulder. His head stopped. Through slit eyes, Tesfahun saw the body laying fifty meters ahead, prostrate as if at rest below a tree of umbrella leaves. His father smiled down on him and they strolled to the tree.

Griffins circled like voracious undertakers and Tesfahun wondered how such things of this world could be. The land and its inhabitants designed by a force unimaginable, mysterious, vapid, yet lurking behind such routine as eating, breeding, dying.

How do they know?

What?

He pointed to the sky. Them.

Kelile looked up. That's how they were made.

But who made them to smell death?

The God of Death has many messengers.

Why would he make them smell death?

Who am I to know the ways of the gods? I am not one of the Kings.

How do they know?

Kelile laughed. You ask too many questions. There are mysteries in this life that just are. The sooner you accept them, the better your life will be. It is how it has always been.

The two walked on in silence yet Tesfahun cared little for lapse.

I hear the elders talking around their fires about the Kangatum. They say we cannot defeat them. That we will lose our cattle.

Kelile kept focus on the kill. The Kings have lost their minds. They speak nonsense.

But aren't they trading with the Sudanese?

It is no matter. They don't know these lands. Our people have been here for generations. Born from the very earth. My father and his. Since the gods created this place. We are the land. Besides, our people have something the Kangatum will never have.

What?

Kelile looked down to his son, a prideful smile upon his lips. His hand smacked the boy's chest, flat against his heart.

Tesfahun looked down at the massive hand and its spreading fingers. But they have guns?

Kelile shook his head and stopped, placing his hand atop his son's scalp. Tessie, my son. There are more things to be afraid of than guns.

Tesfahun nodded. Kelile scanned the area and proceeded walking. Tesfahun ran light-footed to his father's side. The body came closer as they walked.

I saw a woman the other day crying. She was holding her baby like she would never see her again. She kept saying, 'Why' over and over. The next day, I went by and the windows were shut and I heard crying coming from inside.

His father gave no response.

The griffins sat perched in the branches, hesitant at their approach, knowing their place in the natural order. The steps of his father no longer soft but noisome. Kelile's pace quickened. Tesfahun caught up, opened his lips but said nothing as they arrived at the kill.

Kelile unsheathed his blade, crouched over the oryx carcass, slipping the blade from neck to navel, spilling innards onto the darkening dirt. Without inhibition, he began to gut, flinging the insides as the griffins and crows swooped down to collect their bounty. Tesfahun watched, standing idly by like a witness as his father abandoned instruction for efficiency. He wished to help, to learn, but became spectator once again.

Like a butcher, Kelile hoisted the hollow animal onto his shoulders. His white paint reddening on his torso as streams of blood ran down his crescent scars raised across his chest. The hunter turned and followed the trail back south. Tesfahun followed behind. The limp head and those dead-black eyes staring at him as they marched on.

Not until they had resumed the trail by the river did Tesfahun attempt speech again. The river invited the heat yet Kelile kept his gaze toward land, pretending as if the river did not exist. When the landscape became familiar, the boy sped to his father's side. Stern and somber, Kelile walked with his load. Footfalls in the grass the only sound.

Will *əmye* be with us today?

He adjusted the carcass on his shoulders, grunting.

How am I to know what goes on in your mother's head?

They came to the area south to the region of the Crocodile Man's protection. The waters moved with young bodies swimming, splashing downstream. Their dotted shapes visible on the banks ahead as their mothers filled clay pots stationed in the mud. Tesfahun had many things to ask, to talk of, but his mouth stayed sealed by some subconscious rebellion. The family ahead was large, four, five children from one woman. Tesfahun watched the brothers dip under and come up, hands splashing at one another.

Why don't I have a *wändəm!* The thought slipped from his lips.

A massive open palm thundered across his face. The sting flashed across his skin and he raised a startled hand to his cheek, turning from the pleasant scene at the water's edge.

Kelile's eyes beamed down, chest rising and shoulders now bare. Tesfahun gazed through moistened eyes toward his father. A locked gaze empty of any sufficient words. The laughter from the children carried up to them and Kelile's eyes softened. He moved his mouth to speak but no words came.

Turning from his son's eyes, The Great Warrior stooped and swung the oryx over his shoulder again and continued walking, head down, while his lone offspring watched his blurry figure disappear along the river's edge.

II

Outside, Dawit's mother sat on a wooden stool, her hands powdered white with flour. She scraped deep into the carved stone bowl, grinding rock with rock over and over in rhythm. She had a round face despite her body and cool amber eyes that seemed to lift at the corners when she spoke.

Tesfahun approached her and lifted a hand in greeting that she did not see. After a moment, he spoke.

What are you making, Bale?

Her head came up, a momentary wide-eyed look that faded with recognition, before those smiling eyes beckoned welcome.

Oh, Tesfahun, you frightened me.

I'm sorry.

No matter, no matter, she dismissed. She raised the bowl to her face, looking at the boy and smiled, Maize cream.

He leaned, examined the bowl's contents and gave a meek smile.

She laughed through her lips. It tastes better than it looks.

He sat down next to her. Though the same age as his mother, her skin held fast to youth, untouched by the sorrow that etched into Wagaye like river on rock. He watched her with relaxed shoulders, his fist on his chin.

I hear your father took you hunting today.

He shifted. He killed an oryx.

Oh? she said, eyebrows high. Good for him. You know, your father is a skilled hunter. Has he told you of his scars across his stomach?

He shook his head.

He hasn't? Those are from the lion that hangs in your doorway.

Tesfahun straightened. He killed it?

She nodded, a tribal pride gleaming in her features. Her hands continued to work.

Just after his ceremony, he had gone alone to hunt far down the river. When he didn't return that night, we all wondered if maybe he had been killed by Kangatum or maybe the river had taken him. The next morning some of the other warriors were talking of going to search for him. But, as they spoke, we saw him walking toward us, wearing the lion skin like a robe.

Tesfahun imagined the sight of his father, clothed in the lion skin, the mane frilled about his shoulders and those deep scars bleeding down his legs. He wondered if the same bitter expression rested on his face.

I never knew that, he said.

Bale gave a closed lip smile and continued to mash the corn and grains. Even before he could speak, he remembered Bale's Akara stories.

How is your mother?

Tesfahun shrugged, watching her hands as if they were something in his line of sight rather than his mind. His silence piqued her interest and her hands slowed. She let it rest until Tesfahun said, I know what the others say about her.

And what do they say?

He turned his head to the blue sky. That she has a sickness. He tapped his temple with a regretful finger.

She stopped, crouched with the bowl in her white hands. They are fools. You understand?

The flash of insistence in her eyes struck him and he nodded.

She continued mixing the cream. Her bracelets tinkered about her wrists with the motion, loud in the silences between words as they harmonized with the rock. A hag-like cough came from the hut, gurgled and prolonged before ending.

Bale stopped, satisfied, and held the bowl to Tesfahun. Would you take this in for me? My arms feel just as that corn is.

He stood, taking the bowl and eyeing the cream with abhorrence. She stood and wiped her hands across her covering. The collection of beads hung between her breasts and swayed as she walked toward the hut. He followed her in.

Dawit should be inside unless he's out with Dunga.

The hut had no skin but frail shafts of straw hung from the doorframe. Beside two cots on wobbling frames and primitive cookery, the hut held nothing. Dawit's grandmother lay on her back. Her face like a dried plum with two white, veiled orbs just visible. Skin sagged from her bones and her white hair spread long and unkempt. The hut smelled of age but the boy kept his thoughts behind his teeth.

Bale took the bowl from Tesfahun and brought it to the old woman and labored her to a seated position. She mumbled nonsense from her naked mouth before shouting, Bale, is that you?

Yes, yes, mother. I have some food for you.

Where is your father? He's late.

He's dead, Bale said, scooping a fingerful of cream and placing it in her mouth. Her pink tongue flickered about as cream dropped down her chin.

Typical, she remarked with smacking gums.

Tesfahun turned from the sight and, seeing Dawit gone, backed toward the exit.

Thank you, he said, indicating his departure.

Bale looked to him, dropping another glob of cream into her mother's mouth.

Tell Dawit he better be home for supper. And Dunga too. Just because he has a dowry doesn't mean he is not still my son. We will see you at the fire tonight.

Yes, auntie.

He turned, eager to breathe fresh air, but paused when Bale called after him. He turned and her eyes stared straight into him.

She loves you, Little Warrior.
He smiled and walked home.

III

They held their battles outside the village. A grassless area tilled to dirt like some gladiatorial arena, stained with remnants of black blood from fights of their fathers and grandfathers.

He could hear the clack of the sticks and imagine the welts rising on their skins as he approached. Four or five men practiced, some boys who had not had their ceremony. They danced about with sticks raised high. Cuts and raised skin lined their arms and thighs and torso. Some with scars etched into their skin.

One night, Uncle Ogbay, tongue loosed by drink, had told Tesfahun he had once been a stick fighter, known only by a missing tooth and bent pinky, limp save for the bone that gave it form.

Brother instructed brother, the older striking fast and agile while the younger squeaked at the sting. Dawit and Dunga circled. Dunga's reach that of an eagle, moving on timber-like limbs above his small brother. He watched them from the circle, a fraternal bond undeniable. Dawit bore the brunt of the effects. Dunga struck and connected but quick to instruct, demonstrating moves after he performed them.

Tesfahun watched as they ended. Dunga wrapped his lank arm around Dawit's shoulders and both laughed in some state of dejection at some remark his brother had made. Tesfahun kept silent. His thoughts drifted to a fantasy of brotherhood he had never known until Dunga poked Tesfahun's chest back into reality. He staggered awake, rubbing his sternum. Dunga's white smile greeted him back.

What brings you here? Dunga asked. His stick rested on his shoulder like a vagabond.

Dawit held his shorter stick like a staff before him as if he were called to lead his people from bondage. They appeared two of one cloth.

Bale told me to find Dawit.

Ahh, well, now you've found him. A little swollen but still a tough fighter, Dunga remarked with a rustle atop Dawit's head. Dawit squirmed away with an errant slap of his brother's hand.

At least I can beat the Great Warrior's son, Dawit teased, rubbing a welt across his chest with a smile.

Bah, Tesfahun responded, waving a hand. He looked at Dunga. When do you fight again?

It is hard to find anyone willing these days.

What about the Kangatum?

Dunga shifted his stance, spinning his stick in place upon his shoulder.

Those cowards would never fight me. They choose to shoot from the bushes. Jackals with no honor.

They have guns.

What are guns to the Akara? We are the true warriors. Look. See this? he pointed vehemently toward his chest to an elongated series of scars raised on his skin. That was a leopard. And here, a Kangatum warrior who had killed Jima.

He stood proud, sucking a deep breath through his nostrils to extend his chest. No Kangatum will wear my scar.

Dawit chimed, He is the one all the girl's talk about.

Dunga feigned modesty with a dismissive wave. Not all the girls.

Tesfahun pondered his claim. So bold, intrepid of the future, yet knowing not what lay ahead. He thought of how Bale had called him Little Warrior and the emptiness behind such a name.

Your mother wants you home for dinner.

You better run along, Dawit. Go and heal.

She said you too.

Dunga pursed his lips on his tight jaw. He looked to them both then left, stomping child-like homeward, swiping his stick across the border grass. The boys chuckled and strolled behind.

Did you kill one?

Abati did.

He laid his hand on Tesfahun's back. Next time.

They walked each to their own thoughts. The sun hot in the afternoon light like a coat even in their scant garb.

The life of the village was aloft, traveling through the air and bringing the scent of food and sounds of laughter and work. Tick-gorged dogs ran amuck between huts, chased by little ones who clamored at their mangy skins.

Do you remember the rumor?

Huh?

Tesfahun leaned closer as they walked. Of *liji*.

What about it?

The other day, I saw a woman crying and holding her little girl and the next day, she had locked herself inside her hut. No crying noises came from the hut anymore. Like it had never existed.

Dawit shrugged. My mother tells me that it's not important for us to know. They are *mingi* so we should not be concerned.

Tesfahun kicked a small rock and watched it tumble across the dry earth.

What?

I don't know. She says it's a curse. Like bad luck.

But...what happens to them?

The welts on Dawit's upper arms had reddened and he caressed them.

I don't know. Maybe they send them somewhere else to live so their bad luck follows them. She says it's for the good of the village otherwise our crops would die. Our cattle would die or be stolen. The gods punish tribes who house *mingi* children.

One of the mangy dogs, drooling, ran past, the children laughing in blissful hunt like maniacal angels. He watched them run till they rounded behind a staggered fence. Their rounded bellies, ran in uneasy gaits as they moved in the world around them. Innocent and ignorant.

These *mingi* children...

Don't talk about it, Dawit interrupted.

Around the next hut, Bale cooked at a pot, cracking stone upon stone to ignite the dry brush that plagued the land. Dunga leaned over a giant basin, splashing water upon his face. The sparks caught and Bale poured her breath into the spark until the brush ignited in a burst of flame. She nurtured it then rose, clapping the dust from her hands.

Dawit! she exclaimed when she saw him then looked to her oldest who protested silent with palms raised upward. She shook her head and ushered him away. Then she turned and smacked her palm over and over on her eldest's head as he ducked and slid.

Some teacher you are.

If he wants to be a fighter, first he must know pain, Dunga remarked as Bale and Dawit reached the doorway.

Bale's mother sung an old ancient tune Tesfahun had heard once the week of his grandfather's death.

Tesfahun, do you wish to stay and eat? she asked.

No, my father has a kill ready for us.

She acknowledged with a nod. Dawit waved from his mother's shelter, a flush of embarrassment washing his eyes and lips. Tesfahun waived back and turned to head home. Bale's shouts at Dunga faded as he left.

He walked through the village, eyes cast to his feet more than what lay around him. The same faces he knew without the requirement to look. His ears could tell him all that went about him by the scrape of cornmeal upon a bowl or the crackle of twigs for fire. The same shrill voices ebbed the same. He walked past the fence. A new sound came. Strange and inorganic, as if some predator's voice drowned upon some foreign drink. Drawn like to water, small children, some his age, ran their lithe bodies past the fence toward the border of the village. He walked is own pace, neck outstretched and brow dented in curiosity. The noise rolled loud now.

Above the heads of the children, he stared at the large object. Seated atop black, round hoops and growling. Shining and solid but like a box unbreakable. Through the transparent glass, the strange pale faces appeared. White teeth smiled behind their pinkish-red lips. He wondered if they had been bleached by the sun. He had heard of the pale ones but never seen.

It's them, a voice said. He turned to see some of the warriors gather.

A tall woman emerged, coming from an opening within the box. Tesfahun examined her through fascinated and horrified eyes. Her yellow hair swung from under her hat down past her shoulders. Bland coverings fitted across her chest and buttocks. Her massive eyes like large black holes that covered most of her face. The children clamored to them, open palmed and grabbing.

Should we stop the little ones? A warrior asked.

They could see someone behind the glass. A face like theirs. Several others came out, holding little black boxes and holding them to their black eyes as if looking through them.

The strangers wandered around the outskirts of the village, pointing their black boxes at different people, young and old and Tesfahun wondered if they tried to snatch the souls of those they held their boxes to. His eyes could not turn from their teeth, always visible as they passed the children's fervor. They lingered, intrigued, by the young and old girls with plated lips and ears. A man whose hair had begun to fade leaned closer, his pink tongue poked from the side of his lips, and he turned his black box to them.

Behind the hazy window, he could see a dark face, similar to his own. His eyes focused upon objects with no eyes to view. Tesfahun heard the voices raise around him from the villagers.

He's one of us.

Akara?

Kangatum dog.

I can smell their kind any day.

The man behind the glass, dressed as the whites, cast his large pupils at the children, a moue of rancor and fear curled his lips and he shifted inside the machine.

Do the Kings know they are here?

Tesfahun saw his father and several others approach from within the village, decorated with their spears and swords. Bodies smeared white and menacing. The scars across their bodies caught the sun as they came closer. The frantic voices of children and women subsided to a fearful reticence.

Nothing stirred save the white ones and, seeing the ostrich feather and spears, turned their black boxes toward the warriors. Kelile's hand unsheathed his slate sword and brandished the blade before the white ones. Their black boxes dropped, caught by the string around their necks and they stepped back, hands at their heads. The sounds they spoke confused the village, cocking heads and prompting whispers among the groups.

Kelile's voice boomed at them. The woman startled and her lips cringed as her face sunk into itself.

Why do you come here? the Great Warrior asked.

Their eyes comprehended nothing. They searched each other for meaning, but only spoke their own dialect.

Who sent you? he bellowed. A giant foot stomped forward.

The door to the machine opened and the Kangatum man stepped out. His coverings no longer of his tribe, his birth, but tailored to be that of the white ones. His feet, booted and thick, stepped loud past the children and between Kelile and the strangers.

Breath and wind ceased. All stood as still as the boulders of the land, waiting. Breath resumed, a harsh, violent, exhale from the lungs of Kelile. He spoke, low and sober.

Who gave you the right to step on our land? he asked.

The Kangatum smiled, but failed in concealing the fear visible in his eyes. The woman sobbed and one of the warriors hollered.

I have no fight with you, the Kangatum answered.

War is all your people have brought to us.

The Kangatum man pulled the sides of his clothing. I am not like them. See? I don't wear their clothes or fight their wars. I come a new man.

Kelile's eyes stared sharper than his spears. The scars on the Kangatum's chest visible just above his shirt.

Why do you bring them here?

The man looked back at the whites, flush against the vehicle.

They pay me money to let them take pictures. To see the people of the Omo.

Kelile's brow creased.

The man turned and asked in their tongue. The old man nodded and lifted the black box off his neck and handed it to the Kangatum.

Here, the man said, handing the black box to Kelile, it takes pictures.

The Great Warrior examined the black box by turning the cold metal over in his hands. The other warriors crept forward with their eyes affixed to the strange object. Kelile took his fore finger and pressed the button atop the device and it shuttered and clicked. He dropped the box into the dust and swung his blade. The woman with long hair and no eyes let a scream escape her. Kelile's blade raised toward the Kangatum. His eyes wild.

Take them from here.

The oath of my people I don't hold anymore. I live in Addis Ababa now. I mean no...

You think because you wear their clothes, you are no longer a Kangatum dog?

I am not part of that anymore.

Kelile let his eyes search this man before him, an incredulous stare where a decision had to be made. Kelile smirked and stepped close, closer, closer still. His blade rested on the lateral scars on the Kangatum's chest.

You will always be one of them.

Droplets formed on the temple of the man. He closed his eyes as if expecting his fate. Kelile lingered a moment then stepped back. The man's breath returned and he nodded, neither in fear nor acceptance, but nodded. Kelile and the

Warriors began their war chant, pounding their fists against their lean chests.

In a frenzy, the visitors scampered into the machine quicker than they arrived. The growl erupted and the hoops spun atop the slick dust until it fled into the distance, leaving only a brown cloud as the growl waned. But the warriors and their chants still remained.

IV

The villagers spoke of him as if he were a demon. They voiced concerns with a reverent fear of his vigilance and those who joined him into the bush, down river, and into Muhar, Oko, and Kangatum lands. Whether they would return remained unknown though some begged the spirits for his new home to belong elsewhere.

The tribe sat around the large fire, blazing a vibrant, ferocious flame within the stones in the night. Frantic flies and moths came to the flame as if even they had complaints to share as well. Like a wicked séance, they met, man and woman, elder and infant, waiting for the Three Kings to arrive.

Rumors of big cats prowling their borders, spying upon the thinning cattle swept through the owners' conversations. Some of the older claimed a *mingi* was among them. There could be no other explanation. The younger attributed their fearlessness to the whites and their massive machines that ate the land and poisoned the water.

The old sat in dirt or on mats, discomfort seething through their time-worn bones. Ash colored palms rubbed their joints. The younger stood in a circle around the fire. Voices high and low, complaining, fretting, assuring, yet shrouded by confusion. The stark white faces of the painted fighters appeared as floating heads around the circle. Tesfahun scanned the hundreds of faces, feeling the buzz inside. An observant moon watched over the gathering.

Fragments of talk came to him but the meanings remained lost. He could not find his father among the faces. Turning, he looked to his mother and Bale who whispered to one another and laughed. He failed to remember when such a sound came from her lips. A prodding jab nagged his ribs and he shot back with a scowl.

What will the Kings say? Dawit asked.

Tesfahun shrugged.

Across the large fire, he saw her standing with her father and mother and brothers. Though he only spoke to her once by the river, he knew she was called Ayana. His changing body drawn to her though he knew not why.

A sharp jab hit his ribs again.

What?

Dawit pointed.

Tesfahun followed and saw the three round lanterns coming from outside the village. Swaying orbs menacing and solemn in the pitch black until the moon's glow flowed over the relics walking from night.

A gradual hush greeted them. In eternal procession, they marched into the fire glow, following the path between the crowd's circle and emerging into orange and yellow light, *borkotos* in their gnarled, ringed hands. Only the buzz of night insects filled the now silent gathering.

Another figure emerged, towering and lean, painted white and strutting the ostrich feather from the back of his skull. Tesfahun strove to read his father's face but those eyes he could not read.

When the Three Kings had seated themselves upon their *borkotos* in front of the fire and sung their chants of beckon to the spirits in their wavering, broken voices, the oldest King held a hand high, burdened by trinkets about his wrist. His cloudy eyes appeared absent of color in the fire, making his remaining teeth and weathered, droughty skin illuminate in the firelight.

The King lowered his hand.

Akara! This is a difficult time. The Water Spirit has not heard our prayers. Our land is dry. Our animals are dying. And the threat of war has come to our land from those who dwell across the river. But remember, this land has survived for generation after generation after generation. We will endure. The Akara will survive. The Spirits will hear our call but until then, we must practice perfection. Be patient and trust in the Spirits who watch over us.

A brief silence hovered and then a deep voice shouted from the many faces.

How long must we wait?

Who are we to decide? the elder answered.

But our children are starving. We are starving. How long must we wait to watch them pass away?

A woman in the front, her hooped lip dangling to her chin and a newborn suckling at her breast shouted.

We are cursed!

The voices clamored atop each other. Arguments and accusations erupted like a horde of baboons. A momentary bedlam swirled around and Tesfahun the violence of the voices in his muscles. He watched his father stand rigid, close-lipped but strong among the mass of arms flailing. He wished to stand by him and feel his power, let it transfer into his own body. Harness the power he believed lay dormant in his bones.

The tallest king raised his hands beckoning order. A small bone bore through his septum. Even those seated beside him lifted their arms in an almost surrendering gesture. The voices faded.

My people! My people! Hear me! We are a strong tribe. A people who have survived through famine and drought and war. Do you forget when Dula and the Twenty slayed the army of Muhar warriors with only sticks and arrows? Or the prayers answered after the first sacrifice? We are a people of strength. Trust that we have sacrificed enough to gain favor. Have we not fed the river and the Valley for the good of the people?

Grunts of agreement responded.

We have dedicated our many years to the good of you. To the provision of peace among you. To food and family. Pride. Wisdom. We are the mediators of the spirits that could crush us. Sweep our lands away from us. Give us to our enemies. Allow the beasts to overtake our homes and devour our children. But has that happened to you? I ask, have we been given to our enemies? No. Because of our faith, our sacrifices, we have endured and appeased our protectors. What is life without sacrifice? What is life without trials and pain? It is life that brings these to us for if we did not have these, we would have no life. I ask you, all of you, to continue to obey. Respect the spirits. Continue to allow us and pray.

He spoke with fluid movements as if his arms were aided by the spirits themselves. He steadied himself upon a stripped staff longer than his height, adorned with rodent skulls and feathers at its pinnacle. Tesfahun turned to Dawit but his eyes were transfixed on the figures near the flame.

With his eyes back to the solemn crowd, Tesfahun waited for someone to mention the source of their fears. To speak of what all had been simmering about. But no words came and a thick silence settled like a mute fog in the fire glow. Tesfahun's gut danced and, as if his words escaped from his thoughts, he spoke in a loud voice, What about Demissie?

An endless night of eyes looked to him with a terrified gaze. The Kings turned their heads in the direction of the voice, casting a clouded gaze that he felt penetrated his soul. The Kings' lips turned downward.

Who speaks that name?

Murmurs boiled through the crowd. Some pointed and the King turned to face the boy who dared to mention such a name. His towering silhouette backed by the flames stepped toward Tesfahun until he paused. The boy looked up into the shadowy face.

Only death follows such a name. A man forsaken by the spirits and his people. We waste the breath needed to even mention him. We will let him and his pack of wild dogs remain in the wilderness.

Through the fire, he saw his father's gaze fixed at him and he imagined the malicious thoughts brewing behind those eyes. Despite the stares, Tesfahun asked again.

He has taken our best fighters. How can we defend ourselves?

The back of his head tinged with pain. Dawit spoke through clenched teeth in a fervent whisper, Stop.

Why?

Just stop.

Dunga made his choice.

Dawit's eyes flared with a wounded fury. Lips tensed, concealing clenched teeth.

One of the other Kings raised from his stool, leaning heavily upon his staff that rattled. The white, orbital eyes almost shining from a scarified face that appeared saturated in water, shriveled close and pointed. A lank figure, naked save his purple sash across his chest, elevated above his fellow elder. The blind King shook, aiming his useless eyes in the direction of Tesfahun's voice, rage trembling his aged body. The tall King bent and whispered something into the blind King's ear and ushered him to sit.

Raising his arm above the darkness, the tall King spoke to the crowd but Tesfahun knew who the words had been destined for. The words crackled from his lips but so impassioned, all looked upward to this giant apparition.

Concerning the Destroyer, not a thought, nor a word, is to be dedicated to him. Nor his renegade criminals who carelessly wander the bush in search of blood. If our time comes to fight, we will fight. We are Akara and no Kangatum or Muhar will defeat us!

The people seemed satisfied with this answer and chanted We are Akara in thunderous unison. Tesfahun opened his mouth to speak but, feeling the eyes of his father and the tension of Dawit. The Three Kings led the tribe in an incantation for rain and the drums banged an ancient rhythm. The communal voice filled the night and, as the song continued, the Kings exited as they came. Shamans and conjurers returning to intercede for their people. Their lanterns the only wake of their presence.

In clusters, the crowd began to separate, breaking off to their homes while others danced around the fire and sang. A three-legged dog hobbled between the moving groups, sniffing the dirt for scraps usually left by such a gathering. Tesfahun remained as he stood. Disapproving eyes and shaking heads accosted him until his mother patted his bald scalp. He looked to her moist eyes as her malaise guided her home.

The fire still burned. His father looked through the flitting flames into his pupils, leaning against a frenzied fence of shaven wanza timber. His body lax, arms crossed and his face soft. Tesfahun returned the stare. Then walked, feet skidding the earth with head down, to his father's side. He leaned against the same fence and rested his head against the hard wood.

A moment of silence. Then he said, I should learn to not speak.

There is always a time to question. But there's also a time to shut one's mouth.

I don't think I am good at telling time.

It is not a matter of telling time. It is knowing what to ask.

Why wouldn't they answer?

Kelile shrugged his shoulders. Most people don't want to answer if they don't have one.

Demissie is going to start a war for us, isn't he?

Kelile sighed. War did not wait for Demissie. It adopted him.

He straightened and walked. Tesfahun followed, watching his feet and the many footprints laid before him.

Some men seek glory at the expense of others. He cares little for his people. Only for blood.

Aren't men supposed to seek blood?

Real men find ways to avoid it.

They call you 'The Great Warrior' don't they?

He didn't answer. The three-legged dog attempted to raise itself to smote the flame but tumbled onto its back in a small puff of dust.

I don't want to fight.

Kelile sighed as his son sidled next to him in stride. You won't have to. Let's go find your uncle.

Between occupied dwellings, they headed to the sorghum hut, together in solitude, leaving the fire and hearing the distant stuttering yelp of frightened jackals in the outer dark. Behind, the legless dog bayed in response with a foreign voice among such kin.

V

He could hear the voices muffled behind the walls with his father's among them. Outside, he sat and stared from the sparse wilderness where lions lurked in the tall, golden grass back to the path they followed from the village. The hut encircled by a dirt floor where a large fire pit, burnt sticks and charred wood piled high in their destruction where footprints tracked around the stones. Dark blotches remnant of the day spent hunting with his father plopped in no obvious order. He looked to the fence that hung the bleached skulls of jackals, ibex, baboons, griffins. The heads stripped of their natural design and ghostly white. The connective seams pristine of dirt and almost artificial in their posture. Trinkets hung from the heads that he could not identify, bracelets or necklaces sinister in purpose. Perhaps caveats to terrify evil spirits.

He shifted his position, looking over his shoulder at the entrance of the derelict hut. His unease furthered by a phantom chorus of high voices screaming that he puzzled as to whether they were imagined or if they raised in lament from the ground.

When the beaded vines rattled apart, the voices stopped. Kelile walked toward him, heavy browed, determined footfalls stomping past his son to the village. Tesfahun scampered to his feet, slipping as he ran to catch up. The graying skies grew darker and Tesfahun wondered if maybe their dances had worked. Deep gray clouds clashed with white like some slow stew stirred by a mighty hand. He looked back to the distant hut. Three figures stood by the fire pit like aged timbers lurking on the borders of another realm, gathering to continue their prayers and ceremony.

The ostrich feather jutted skyward, fluttering in the wind.

What did they want? Tesfahun asked.

Kelile spat into the grass. Ahhh... he remarked with a wave of his hand. Old fools. Stubborn old fools.

The words came out slow as if dragging anger. Tesfahun tried to see his face but his steps were too quick.

Do we have to?

No.

No? What about our cattle?

It is our problem.

But you said the Kangatum...

I know what I said, he barked, turning abrupt to face his son.

That bellowing voice rang into his ears and down to his stomach.

Tesfahun dropped his eyes and waited till his father resumed his march homeward. He followed the same path, placing his tracks within his father's as the sky only darkened.

They arrived at home to find two women seated inside, sitting on the floor, each sipping at a cup of tea. Wagaye faced the other. She turned her face to the men and Tesfahun saw her eyes, puffy and tired.

How did it go? Wagaye asked, her lips hovering just above the lip of the cup. Steam coiled before her face.

Who is this? he snapped.

She smiled a weak smile.

Louam. A friend.

Kelile's wild eyes scanned each woman as if trying to decipher some scheme about to befall him. He reached over and grabbed his bow and a handful of arrows.

I'll be back before sundown.

He moved toward the door. Tesfahun motioned to follow but his father nudged his forearm into his son's chest with a grunt, muscling his way through the lion's skin. He watched the skin swing till it resumed its motionless post.

Tes, come here.

He faced his mother and knew to come forward yet he stood still. Legs incapable of movement. He watched the other woman and felt a nostalgic sorrow familiar to his life. Two of the same were before him. The same haunt his mother harbored had become hers to bear as well.

I want you to meet a friend.

She beckoned for him with soft waves of her hand. He approached them and stood close to his mother. The other woman looked forlorn at him, eyes canvassing his features. He saw a tear slide from her eye.

Hello, Tesfahun.

He nodded then felt a hand rubbing the small of his back. Wagaye's hair had been combed and now seemed more kept than previous days. And he saw a compassion, empathy unknown, kept from his viewing in her eyes.

Speaking to the other woman, still rubbing his back, she said, This is my son. Growing so fast. Soon to be a man.

Such a handsome boy. Like his father. You must be proud, the woman remarked, concealing her lips with the cup.

The rubbing slowed and then stopped. He stood between the two, both reminiscing in their own worlds. No longer talking but wallowing together for each other's separate miseries.

May I go? he asked.

She looked at him. A mild terror seized her before she answered, Why don't you stay? It's nice to have you here.

But I wanted to go...

Not now.

There was a finality in her words that he obeyed, shuffling slump-shouldered to the cot and lifting the mattress to retrieve his palette and canvas to draw alone.

He sat with his tools upon the bed. Grey light shone through the window, illuminating him in a morose glow. He took his index finger and applied an earthy tone to the bare canvass, dragging his fingertip with a delicate purpose. The outline of some hidden image traveled from his mind to his fingers in some desperate need to live. Head down and mind elsewhere, he listened as the two women spoke.

It is difficult now but, in time, things will get easier. His mother's voice the voice of a heart invested to another's sorrow, desiring restoration, he could not tell. Have you cleansed at the gate?

The other woman's voice cracked and she wept in deep sputtering moans and he knew that mourning. Raising his eyes, he looked and knew her face. Now childless but here, in his home, with his family, weeping as his mother's frail arms enveloped her and awkward in her embrace. A face older than the days before, glistening in the grey light.

My girl, she lamented. Wagaye pat her back, rocking to the rhythm as if they both danced a helpless dance to the fate of all life.

Knowing of what could happen is not the same as it happening to you. My own child. My own daughter.

It is for the better of the village, Wagaye assured.

How could something so pure carry such an evil? Even after my time at the gate, I feel the curse still with me, the woman moaned.

Wagaye said nothing but instead hummed a song, culling this stranger like her own blood. His finger stopped on the canvas and the heat flushed to his face. The longer he stared, the warmer his skin became until he slammed his canvas upon the soft mattress and left. He pushed the lion skin aside and left without protest or notice.

In his anger, he had arrived at Dawit's, standing outside the quiet hut. He walked to the door and peered through the beads then turned back to the yard. The fire pit lay cold to his right.

Abandoned pots and spoons crusted over as flies buzzed. He sat on a rock, watching the ash and the charred remnants of better times now burnt to memory and he imagined the family a family, not captive to some unknown division as elusive as wind.

Dreams filled him and he stretched his legs, splaying his toes. His mother sat to his right, laughing full but mute, and his father, relaxed and dancing like some jester for the pleasure of his blood. Her eyes squinted, soft tears leaking down her smile as she watched the Great Warrior's comic steps, arms popping like a wounded bird. She turned her gaze toward him, a love exhausting to bear lifting her lips. Tesfahun smiled as Kelile leaned over, falling into her and kissing her forehead and cheeks, not only lovers but friends, teasing only as love would allow. The grey light blurred behind their figures and his mother looked to him and she spoke in a foreign voice. The voice came not from her lips but outside of her.

Tes?

The world spun until his eyes saw sky and his back thumped into the dirt. A face blocked his view of the sky for a brief moment before Dawit's face blocked the sun.

What are you doing?

Nothing.

A concerned yet urgent wildness filled Dawit's face and he stepped close enough for Tesfahun to feel his breath in his ear.

I found it, he whispered.

What?

I'll show you.

Where? What about your mother?

Do you want me to show you or not?

Dawit gestured with his head, insistent eyes spoke his impatience. He dusted himself off with a brush of his hand and followed Dawit's lead.

The two kept silent as they passed between huts and fires, sleeping elders and playful children in the quiet morn. Each face presented itself to Tesfahun as a spy and his heart beat like a deep drum at each glance. Dawit walked with his head high and Tesfahun tried to mirror his friend but fretted over being found out as an imposter.

A black and white dog burst from behind a fence, barking as two girls pursued. Tesfahun startled back and the girl's laughed in passing. His eyes followed them and when he faced forward,

Dawit vanished around a corner. He quickened, tripping over roots and rocks while he passed the boundaries of the village into the unknown thickets.

Fighting branches and thorns, he followed the sounds of Dawit's wake, catching glimpses of a foot, a hand, a back. His heart beat frenzied now. A paranoia set in his arms and legs.

He heard himself call for his friend, the voice muffled within the dry foliage. The scrapes and stings of this wilderness, this unknown darkness, suffocated him. The unmistakable desire for the glimpse of an open plain, to see light and life and not be choked by the fear of death. He shouted to Dawit in shaky terror and surged forward, teeth grit to aching, until he felt himself collide with a soft body and tumble into the coarse grass.

He righted himself and saw Dawit over him with an outstretched hand. Breath pounded in his lungs as he sat upright.

Do you need to rest?

Tesfahun tried to speak but only nodded.

How many times am I going to have to pick you up? His playful smile eased the fear in his veins.

Your mother will beat you for this, Tesfahun warned.

She can beat me but she can't own me.

A determined defiance swelled in Dawit's eyes.

You don't have to prove yourself. Not to me. Tesfahun said.

The defiance gleamed even stronger in Dawit's eyes. Come on.

The two walked a newly trampled path, surrounded by tall, skeletal trees among the round bursts of brush. The path was empty of life and Tesfahun felt as if he had entered a path that led to a commune where life should not dwell.

How did you find this path?

I heard your Uncle Ogbay speak of it, down at the sorghum hut.

Tesfahun said nothing.

I didn't drink anything. I hid outside, listening.

A soft breeze blew. Neither warm nor cold. Tesfahun glanced back and saw only the darkness of the bush. Dawit began to bite the nail of his thumb and Tesfahun noticed.

You haven't been here before, have you?

Dawit shook his head, presenting himself as fearless but unable to hide his tells.

What did Ogbay say about this place?

Dawit's usual voice subdued to a timid whisper. When you told me of that woman, I became curious. So I snuck around the old huts listening to the elder's stories. I had heard Dunga mention something about the Valley of Dry Bones before he left. Ogbay said the same thing.

Tesfahun's white eyes widened. This leads there?

Dawit shrugged. We'll find out.

Does Dunga know?

He would lash me for going here. But he chose to leave.

They walked on, ducking past some low, solid branches ahead.

How much further?

I don't know. Shut up.

Ahead, the path became closed with brush and overhanging limbs. A speck of light appeared. The trampled path established itself. The earth compacted underneath their bare feet.

Tesfahun followed until Dawit paused at the threshold and glanced back at his friend. Droplets slid down his temples. The breath came fast through his nostrils. His fertile mind's eye envisioned a land where the dead roamed, animal and human alike. The rumors of this place resurrected to memory behind his eyes. A lawless place where the living had no warrant to walk and those who dwell there, in this forbidden land, bore down upon trespassers like crows on carrion, stripping the mightiest men of the futile attributes they bore with a surreptitious ease, leaving these once powerful to the mercies of the dead where there is no hierarchy, no order.

We should leave, Tesfahun advised.

Not now, Dawit turned.

The clouds had thickened, casting a darker gray across the land and Tesfahun looked to the sky as if something may strike them.

Come on, Dawit commanded in a weak tone. He pushed through the bush and disappeared. Tesfahun swayed, the weight rocking on the edge of his feet before closing his eyes and pushing through the stabbing branches.

He knew he had emerged on the other side but his eyes failed to open. No longer branches or thorns but a vast silence before his closed eyes. He could hear Dawit's breath and nothing more.

Reluctant, his lids lifted.

His vision focused upon a descending plain of dry dust, cracked stone, and debris spread like gravel across the terrain. Nothing grew nor stirred and the two boys, so valiant in their former courage, stood like lost children before the fangs of a lion. Tesfahun's breath held, then poured from his open mouth in unmetered rhythm.

Dawit's limp hands hung at his side as he descended the steady decline of the dusty path. Steps soft as whispers.

Tesfahun reached out to grab his Dawit's arm but missed, nearly tumbling over.

Dawit continued without a glance and Tesfahun followed Dawit's lead. His mind shouted for him to return home, to be a good boy. But he marched forward.

The dust plumed at the slightest step, leaving an ethereal wake behind them. The dying grass's life departing as they drew closer to the barren plain. A desolation inconceivable spread at their feet. Tesfahun looked back to the shelter. The salty taste atop his lips. He watched himself, walking into this land of myth few spoke of. Two figures as alien as life in the land where the Kings stole when night fell. He wondered what sacred rite was performed here. The gods pacified by what religious sacrifice was offered. For a brief moment, he wondered if, perhaps, the myths only existed in the mind and nothing but dust dwelled where they stood.

The path leveled. He looked back to the brush, now distant on the rise. The shelter waned and the dust rose and the plain now upon their feet. The few basket-sized stones lay sporadic till they disappeared in the horizon.

Dawit continued, ever silent but determined drove forward in hopes of discovering an ancient secret no one would validate. Tesfahun stopped at the threshold, his feet sunk in the powder, soft but mingled with jagged pebbles. He looked down at his feet and recognized a trinket from the Kings. A thin rope adorned with the teeth of jackals, separated by rounded, blue beads. An omen his father said to ward off death in all its forms.

Tesfahun had almost reached Dawit when he felt pressure underfoot. The cracking noise sounded grotesque to Tesfahun yet he knew not why, for he had never heard such a sound. The pressure turned to pain and he stepped back, eyes to the earth. Partially buried in the dust, the remnants of shattered bones lay around his foot. The knobby, fleshless fingers reached from their shallow grave. He bent down and examined the shards and reached down and exhumed them from the dust. His lungs broke and he dropped the stained artifacts back to their grave. The five fingers lay visible atop the dust, small enough to fit into Tesfahun's palm.

His heart pulsed blood through his veins. Eyes unable to turn from the earth. The adrenaline dumped into his legs and he ran to Dawit.

It's true, Dawit. It's...it's...

Dawit raised solemn eyes to his friend, mouth agape and arms listless. Whatever determination resided in his friend had been snatched from him.

What?

Dawit returned his eyes to what held him in that place.

What is it?

Tesfahun looked then fell to his knees. Palms placed to his eyes. An unholy breeze blew, swirling clouds of dust around them, dancing like demons across this dry valley littered with the skulls of cursed children.

The breeze blew in their ears, their eyes, their bones. A lonesome sound for a lonesome land. Blurred shapes appeared on the horizon. Winged caretakers flew soundless above, aloft in patient circles. Fearful of life's visitation. The remains of scat littered at their feet.

They scanned the valley floor and the countless bones it held. Femurs. Newborn skulls. Ribs. Teeth. Scattered fragments like a morbid puzzle abandoned. A hollow moan echoed through Tesfahun's spirit. His eyes did not see what lay before him and his mind wandered to the whispers he had heard as a child.

The rumors of the Kings and of disappearing children.

Mingi.

Harbingers of famine and drought and war.

Children infected by evil spirits, condemned to the Valley.

Mingi.

So many cursed, so many left to return to dirt.

They did not know how long they lingered. In time, they helped each other and walked the path that led them. Passing the silent epitaphs of the disposed to return to the land of the living where they felt unworthy to return. Behind them, they could hear the rustle of those who preyed upon the dead returning to their feast but they would not look back.

VI

$\Large A$t night, he sat close to the fire as the argument continued from earlier. Their voices ebbed behind the lion skin, muffled and nondescript.

The fire's warmth tickled his skin. His gut loaded with flatbread and stew empty of game. The taste now nostalgic to his lips. Deserted lands forced the hunters to traverse farther, only to return later never having released an arrow. The despondency in the warrior's faces as they returned forced the reality they must rely upon the dry soil. A gamble the Akara wished to bypass.

The volume increased as the voices grew deeper, vehement and tireless. His attempts to let his mind wander only returned him to the Valley days ago. A stain upon his memory. The silent voices cried in his ears. Their thoughts, their fears, their questions. Such a multitude of forgotten voices bereft of ears to hear them. He focused on the real voices coming from his home. His name from his mother's lips then diminished to murmurs. He adjusted his position, letting the blood flow through his cramped legs.

Rubbing the remnants of his flatbread between thumb and finger, he watched the fire glow. The violence and fury captivated him a moment. An element bestowing life and stealing the same gift it gave. Such mysteries abound the earth cannot comprehend what it beholds. He bit a small chunk and the chewed food stuck to his gums and teeth but nothing could quench his thirst. The cisterns held nothing but the memory of fresh water.

Lost in thought, he heard a voice startle him back.

What are you doing, boy?

Kelile looked down on his son then out into the darkness beyond their home. Tesfahun heard the soft whimpers from the hut and he looked but saw no face in the window.

Kelile stared off. The crackle of flames and splitting wood became deafening static under the stars. Tesfahun nipped another morsel of flatbread as Kelile tossed the kindling into the fire. The wood clacked and sparks showered on the dirt. The lights above, luminous and infinite, marked the blackness from horizon to horizon, catching Tesfahun's eye as he marveled at these orbs, so distant and free, witness to the earth's life. Witness to such wonders and atrocities unimaginable.

Not a sole stirred within the village. Embers, the only remaining remnant of life, grasped at their heat. The two appeared like wanderers into some damned village haunted by the long dead. Such isolation squeezed Tesfahun's innards. A jackal laughed in the darkness but his father's black eyes did not move.

Kelile's cheeks, once rounded and smooth, now pulled with some weight, down his skull. Creases like canyons split from his nostrils to the edges of his lips. Caked with war-like patterns and scars too numerous to count. Daily becoming an ancestor of the land, no longer a warrior but a sage whose wisdom empowered him.

With a grunt, Kelile sat atop a wanza stump across from the fire and looked through the flames at his child.

Are you ready to receive your scars? he asked.

Tesfahun's bones shuddered at the words, but nodded a false courage. He rubbed his smooth skin and, in comparison to the image across the fire, he felt naked and alien to his own kind. Kelile reached for a branch and prodded the fire. Across the fresh sparks, Tesfahun witnessed a sorrow on his father's face. The once stern, stoic expressions had softened in the fire glow and a great burden seemed to keep him seated on the wanza stump.

Listen to me, son.

Tesfahun straightened, resting his head on his palms.

Kelile let out a deep sigh before speaking.

The elders and gods have doomed us. Belief will end us. What god, what spirit, allows such drought and famine for his people? Why strive to please such a thing that does nothing for so much sacrifice? I am an old man, Tes. A man who may not see if these people, this village, you, will live a happy life. From what I have seen...what I have done, my heart tells me time is shortening. Your mother...

He stopped, then clearing his throat. She will not return. How could she? How could I? It has been so long.

His eyes glazed. He gave a crude wipe at his nose then spat into the fire.

Time is the greatest enemy.

Now on the verge of manhood, Tesfahun saw The Great Warrior infected by a pestilent grief. The same his mother dwelled in.

I am ready to fight for our land, Tesfahun lied.

His father raised his eyes and studied his progeny.

I used to be as you are now. So eager to run into the bush to confront danger. Blood became my worth.

He rubbed his callous hands along the scars on his chest. Slow, delicate movements as if each accessed a memory. Moths began circling erratic loops near the flame.

Do you know of your grandfather?

Tesfahun shook his head.

Kelile adjusted his position and leaned forward as he spoke.

Things were not much different. We had our wars. Our dry seasons. Yet we still had hope. Your grandfather was a good man. A powerful man who would swim with the crocodiles to test them. He cared for us, for his people and sought peace but would fight if he had to. Just like he did with Iskinder long ago. Like you will someday. Me and Ogbay admired him for that. I was your age when he was ambushed on a hunt by a Kangatum man near the river. Pierced with seven arrows and left to rot. A debt to be settled for the body of another Kangatum killed by our tribe. To be eaten by griffins and jackals like game. I watched them bring his body back to the village on wanza boards. It took four men to carry him.

The fire spoke in the brief silence.

At first, I felt nothing. I couldn't hear Ogbay crying or mother moaning. My younger brothers, just children, did not understand. All life vanished from me. But then the wrath came. I thought of how father must have felt when he knew he was to die. I pictured the man who killed him and how his breath sounded before striking the death blow. What fear my father felt. A good man as him did not deserve a death like that. And no longer did it become my duty to avenge him, but my obsession. I needed to find the Kangatum dog who had made me and Ogbay bastards.

His body tensed as the memories came back to him. Tesfahun watched his hands grip the stick prodding the fire as if it had shapeshifted into a weapon.

After we had mourned seven days, I left. Before mother or Ogbay had risen and went east to across the river. I arrived before I was aware. Not a fear but a rage sustained me, drove me. No thought of mother nor Ogbay or my younger brothers. Of my own death. Just of blood. I sat inside the bush for hours. Waiting. Watching. Night fell and I waited. Birds mistook me for branches and perched on my shoulders.

And then I saw him. Alone and stumbling from a hut drowning in drink. At first, I did not know it was him but as he came closer to the bush to let his water out, I saw my father's sash. It was then I knew hate, Tessie. Something blinded me then and when my eyes were reopened, he lay at my feet and I on top of him. He was still alive and clutching his belly to keep his bowels from falling out. No one around but us in the darkness. It smelled of piss and blood and sweat. My palms glistened in the distant village light but, in the darkness, it reminded me of water. And he looked up at me.

His eyes. I had never seen eyes as those. He tried to speak but I ran the knife across his throat and listened to his words drown.

Tesfahun realized his hands had become clammy and he felt the ache through his joints. His father seemed propped by invisible wires as he spoke.

I had taken his life for a life but what had I accomplished? Was I a man now? He rubbed his fingertips gently across a sequence of bubbled scars on his cheek.

You did your duty as the oldest, Tesfahun remarked.

I was just a boy.

Tesfahun paused. I would kill for you.

Never kill for me! he snapped, raising a poignant finger at his son. Tesfahun flinched at the rough order from deep within his father's soul.

Kill for nothing and no one. These scars mean nothing. Nothing, understand? Look at me! I am no longer a man.

You are a good man.

Demissie was right...

You are not Demissie.

How am I not?

Tesfahun paused, appearing at a loss of response then said, Demissie is a *reb*.

He looked to his son with wide eyes, then a comical smile spread across his face. He made no attempt to prohibit him from the sight of his father battling tears. He reached across the dwindling fire and squeezed Tesfahun's shoulder and waited, perhaps to speak more than he had allowed himself, but stopped.

Without warning, he stood. Tesfahun followed and when they both were standing, Kelile looked into his child's face and examined it. Red eyes and a sad smile on his lips but prideful in its features. No words passed.

Kelile turned and walked past him toward the village, leaving him standing alone between his home and the village. The pained figure walked past the crude fences, quiet huts, and dead fires until he disappeared among the homes of his people.

VII

At sunrise, Tesfahun awoke to find his father gone and his mother weeping. He raised himself from the floor and watched her huddled in mourning. Her whimpers bounced from the mud walls and bubbled like rain drops as he gathered himself for the day. He opened a clay pot and retrieved a piece of stale flatbread. Taking a bite, he informed his mother of his departure and emerged into daylight.

The sun hung in the sky just above the scattered treetops, still burning off the orange glow of its slumber. He walked through the village among the few awake who crouched around their fires and readied their meals. A pack of dogs stood outside a broad-shouldered man's home, rummaging through a pile of semi-fleshed bones from an oryx. He wondered where he may have found that animal. The vulnerable words he spoke the night before at the fire still fresh in his thoughts.

When Dawit's hut appeared, he slowed. The windows remained shut and a foreign silence lingered. He crouched and hovered his palm to find the fire cold. As he neared the doorway, he could hear the unmistakable whimper of a mother's sorrow. A sonorous heave with each labored exhale. His feet crept of their own accord. It was not until Dawit's voice broke the silence that he breathed again.

The boy before him was not his friend, but a shell of him. He stood slump-shouldered and hanging like an abandoned puppet. His drooping eyes showed through his painted face.

What happened? Tesfahun asked.

His voice came but as a breath, loud enough for Tesfahun to decipher the words and weight their reality with the utmost urgency.

Who is dead? he asked.

Dawit did not answer but cringed then hiccupped tears down his cheeks. The answer came from within the sorrow and the news affected Tesfahun like some drug struck his body making the world spin and his knees loose.

No, no, no, he repeated over. When?

Dawit snorted, wiping his nose. Two days ago.

Tesfahun approached Dawit and was pulled forward and those lithe arms engulfed him and his sorrow moaned for the loss. His mind swirled inside him like a vortex of memory. Flashes of Dunga's tall figure. Stick held upon his shoulder. Laughing with an arm around Dawit's neck. Telling jokes around the fire pit. The echo of his singing echoed along the paths of the village.

The two embraced as the emotions drained from them. Tesfahun stood back, wiping his face with both sides of his hand.

Does your mother know?

He nodded, pointing toward the wilderness, under a wanza tree's shade. He squinted and saw the shade of a figure in repose as it rocked in a manner Tesfahun recognized from his own mother.

Who did it?

Kangatum, he answered distant.

Tesfahun sat on the earth and folded his knees to his chin. Dawit continued to stand but eyes only for his feet as if the weight of light were too much for him to bear.

When his head had cleared, Tesfahun realized the absence of sound, of people, from the village, and he understood.

Do we have the body?

Dawit nodded without words to match such grief.

He sprung to his feet and sprinted to the far-end of the village. His pace increased as he weaved through silent huts until his body pulsated toward the hallowed ground set apart in the wilderness. He felt the drum-like pound of his pulse in his temples. He passed the border, passed the mingi gate, and followed the empty path that led through tall grass. The sea of yellow stalks brushed his bare legs and the beads around his wrists and ankles shook like some frenzied tribal percussion. Closer and closer he came, seeing the sundry skulls and trinkets and the black doorway to the hut.

Life stopped at the doorway. He stepped quiet as he entered in, giving no heed to the presence of the Kings or the heavy darkness. He did not notice the stench of mold and decaying flesh from slaughtered animals, nor the colored powders in clay bowls lining the shelves floor to ceiling, nor the crocodile head hanging like some grotesque chandelier from the pitched roof.

He had eyes for only the body.

The skin torn by the beaks and jaws of scavengers and pierced by the Kangatum's guns. His head and torso, so decimated by their hatred, he could not know for sure if the body on the table belonged to Dunga. He stared at the body on the floor, drifting away from sorrow and pain and rage and blood lust.

A man sidled next to him. Without raising his eyes from the body, he knew his father's presence. The voices of the Kings chanted a plea to the spirits to avenge Dunga's killer and guide his soul to the peaceful land all warriors will see where there is no drought or famine or hunger. Their ancient voices, low and broken, sung their pagan canticles as Kelile ushered him out the door.

Outside, the light shone bright and disrespectful of the dead. They walked from the hut with the meager voices still pleading to the gods.

It is a terrible thing.

Tesfahun cradled next to his father's hard ribs. Both so thin, their bodies felt like bone upon bone.

A messenger came in the night and asked me to meet him. I went to the river and told Bale. Dawit was there as well. This is a terrible thing.

Tesfahun grasped his temples with his palms, shaking his head back and forth with no purpose. Black birds loitered in the neighboring brush, perched atop an amputated tree, cawing and shrieking like some morbid mob.

Dunga had gone alone, Kelile remarked. According to the other men, he told no one. He attempted to ambush a Kangatum at night in his hut but when he entered, the man was waiting for him. I don't know how he knew but he was ready. They heard the shots and followed but they would not risk more deaths by entering the village. They waited till light and his body was found in some tall grass, covered in crows and flies.

Kelile watched and waited for his son to speak but no words came.

I know this hurts. Even more so for Dawit. But that is war. Our destiny we cannot flee from. A tragic destiny I wish was not ours. But now is not the time to dwell. Vengeance must be taken and it is Dawit's to take.

More blood? Tesfahun cried.

The words his father spoke came rote as if the very syllables held no meaning. A surrender lingered among the sounds. He did not stop looking at his son as he spoke them.

It is better to die than to live without killing.

Is it? Tesfahun asked.

Kelile stared his burdened eyes at his son.

Go home, he said and returned to the King's hut and the darkness leaving Tesfahun to sit like some boneless carcass heaped upon the earth.

His body and spirit made no attempt to stand, nor move, nor think. He sat as a body in time, combating the cauldron of emotions firing upon him like hail. Despite his defense, he failed to stop the thoughts of Bale and Dawit. Nor could he stop the voices of the mingi children in the Valley, or the imagined cry of Dunga as death took him. Hatred brewed, welling beneath the pain and sorrow. Hatred for the Kings, for the spirits, for his parents, for his ancestors. A vitriol against their songs sung throughout his childhood. Those malevolent birds, black as hell, loitering to devour his friend's brother already victim of a most violent end.

One crowed. He fumbled around him, keeping a dagger-like stare on the closest and wrapped his fingers around something hard and flung it forward. It fell well short. The bird's fluffed their wings, danced on the naked limbs, then settled again ready to do the work they had been made for.

VIII

Dunga's body remained among the trinkets and bones for seven days. The Kings prayed for his spirit and sprinkled powders to combat evil that may hinder his crossing. The village continued their daily activities and the men maundered about, returning empty handed from futile hunts. The mothers, clung to by their children, ground grains for short bursts only to quit. Since Dunga had not sought approval from the Kings, his body would not be buried.

The body had been wrapped tight in white linens and carried by men whom he had spilled blood with from the sacred chambers of the King's hut. Dawit and Tesfahun walked on either side of the processional. Dunga's renowned stick, longer than his body, lay tucked against his side and held in place by a stationary hand. Arms shouldered the dead weight of his torso as they approached a mass of sober painted faces who stood in a circle by the mound of sticks and grass.

The Kings came from behind. The strongest bore a flickering torch even more vibrant than the evening sun. The sky blazed afire, pocked by patches of clouds. Closer they marched to the congregation and, when the rigid carapace that once housed Dunga's spirit was seen, the wailing songs began. A chorus sung an aching melody. One that intoned of their loss and pleaded with the pantheon of gods to protect their native son on his final journey.

The voices traveled to their ears and Tesfahun's torpid hatred revved inside. He looked to Dawit's downcast face and saw only a numb boy aching. His brother's body emitted a malodorous aroma of decay and cleansing root. Through the linens, only the shadow of Dunga's body could be seen.

The crowd became more distinct and the first he saw was Ogbay, surrounded by those who partook with him in his frequent escapes. His paunch hung over his covering, painted in white stripes across his body. By his stance, Tesfahun knew he had abstained for this event and wondered how long he could last before returning to the sorghum hut. He could see his eyes, tinted an unnatural yellow.

They stood a few feet from the pyre when a cry rose above the chorus. A groan of no parallel that unearthed from deep within a fractured soul that bore the loss of a husband and sons given to their rightful duty.

Bale flailed on her knees as if bowing. Her palms flat in the dirt. Ash coated her dark skin in a silver gray from scalp to sole, naked save her waist covering. The song continued but her pain haunted his heart. He tried to focus on something else. The living or the dead. His mother knelt next to Bale with her arms wrapped around her waist, face pressed into her side. The two mothers emptied their grief before creation.

The processional stopped but the songs continued. The Kings took lead and stood at the readied pyre before them. They began chanting in unison, asking the spirits to embrace Dunga as an Akara warrior. Tesfahun attempted to ignore their morose prayers yet their trembling, ancient voices stoked his anger. He scanned the crowd, looking for Ayana but could not find her. A sinking feeling entered his heart and the ghostly songs and chants swirled in his ears.

Deeper and darker the sky became and the torches burned as if fueled by the chants. The Kings finished their exhortations and the body was laid upon the pyre. Dawit gazed forlorn and glassy-eyed at his brother and Tesfahun put an arm about his shoulders but felt no life in his friend.

The blind King mumbled under his breath and stepped next to the boys. He extended the torch toward Dawit who received it like a reluctant gift. He held the torch at his waist and stared at the body. Bale's wails lifted above the songs again. He leaned in closer and closer until the flame licked the brittle wood. The flame gathered and spread, devouring the white linen and the body it held.

Dawit began to sing with the others, a whisper but just enough to be heard. Tesfahun could not bring himself to lift his voice. The melody started in his gut and climbed upward till he felt the heat behind his cheeks and forehead. Flames danced above the body with a plume of dark smoke curling heavenward. The crackle of wood and flesh simmered. A pungent burning filled the area and the dogs sniffed wildly at the air. Darker the sky became. Dunga's stick burned against his charring body, the linens melting into the shaft.

His heart burned rivaling the fire. He attempted to force his mind to remember times with Dunga but only his thoughts only called upon the Demissie the Destroyer. He imagined what his face looked like. The impious features hovered like a decapitated demon in his eyes and a consuming desire to strangle this improvident deserter simmered. He poured his blame into that it. Those black pupils, broad nose and bald head, scarred with lives beyond number. But he wondered if the thirst for blood only existed in his rage.

The Kings turned, scooping their *borkotos*, and walked past the now only child, gesturing their condolence. Their arthritic hands protruded from under their purple cloths with jingling wrists. Bare mouths murmured in the orange glow. Dawit gave them a vacant gaze, still held upright by Tesfahun's arm. Each before leaving cast a secondary scowl toward Kelile's boy. Tesfahun imagined only rancor etched in those eyes, those lips, those bat-like ears. A trio of false clairvoyants.

The Three slinked off as well as their bodies would allow. The song still carried through the air, even from Dawit's lips. Some mothers pounded their heads with their palms and men pumped fists into their stolid chests.

He looked to his father, mouth moving to the song.

To Ogbay, mouthing the words he could remember.

Wagaye, leaning her temple to Bale's as they both sang the elegy, cradled into one another like one mourning plant entwined.

But he could not sing.

He searched again for Ayana, for that round, dimpled face. A semaphore among a sea of darkness but he could not find her. The tears welled and he grimaced against them only to fail.

The sound ended and then silence. A moment lingered in the fresh night and the pyre's massive height had subsided to a steady burn. All waited until a strong man Tesfahun recognized as Ayana's father stepped forward before the flame and spoke in a voice lower than the grave.

I have known many men in this village. Many who have died in the midst of war. But I tell you this, I had never known a better fighter than Dunga. His fighting, his skill, was like the sweetest drink. One could get lost in his movements during the stick fights that we often forgot a fight was happening. But what I will miss most of all, is that white smile he always carried. His fearless heart. His love for his brother and his family. I will not speak of the deserter. Though we all secretly scorn him in our hearts. But these few words are all that will be addressed about him for this is a time to remember a fallen warrior.

He turned toward Bale, still shrouded by Wagaye's brittle frame.

We all knew Dunga received from you courage, compassion, and devotion. All you have endured, such loss, will be greatly rewarded. Mourn now, sister. Grieve, but know your sons and husband dwell in splendor, accompanied by the great spirits.

The crowd gave a grunt of approval. Bale did not respond, in voice or gesture, content to let the sorrow consume her as the fire devoured another Akara son.

Others stepped forward and spoke comfort and hidden memories that held a sense of veracity and whim but always a tinge of lore. Another stick fighter came forward and praised Dunga's skill while a young woman known to be infatuated with him attempted to recollect but succumbed to her tears. Tesfahun listened but faded. The words entered his ears but his mind rejected them, much too concerned with what torpor brewed within him. The stories sounded rehearsed and he eyed each speaker with narrowed eyes.

The stories Tesfahun did absorb seemed familiar to him as if he had heard these at a similar event. Valorous escapades of courage and fight but not of Dunga's hands. But such a young mind could not recall and he felt the muscle of Dawit's bicep as he squeezed. He loosened his grip, wriggling the fingers to life again. Dawit paid no mind and only stared at the pyre's dance. Tesfahun looked at his friend and whispered, Don't seek vengeance.

Now his eyes turned, looking upward into Tesfahun's face but nothing came behind them. No fear, nor anger, nor vengeance. Only hollow portals into nothingness as if his soul lay imprisoned. Another speaker came forward and began but Tesfahun pat Dawit's shoulder and turned his back upon them, walking away from the glow and witnessing his own shadow precede him.

Tesfahun, a voice called.

He turned and saw Dawit facing him, illuminated from behind and turning him to a silhouette. Neither cared to speak nor move and Tesfahun felt an instinct to accompany his friend in this hour but he could neither return nor depart. His feet had grown roots like the ancient trees of this land. Or had they?

Looking at Dawit, he believed all the eyes were upon him, awaiting his decision. All eyes save those of his mother. His gut boiled and his roots upended and he turned into the darkness. The fire dwindled behind him till he stood alone at his hut on the border of wilderness and civilization. He entered the lion skin and fell onto the cot that smelled of his mother alone and he ached for the fear of losing his friend.

He wept, only seven days from the ceremony, and, as he let the tears drip down his face to mingle with the dried sorrow of his mother's upon the cot, he felt not a man but a boy in a man's world. He lay on his back, looking to the textures of the hut's roof. The air thickened in his lungs and he knew he this place held nothing for him. He stood and left, looking skyward to the illuminations and the great moon above him.

He scanned the skies and, searching to see if these gods would ever show their face before whispering his decree.

I hate your ways and your sacrifices. Your demands. You always ask but never give. Now you have taken someone close to me. And now, because of you, the one closest to me like a brother will die. Because of you and your laws. Spirits, listen to me, for now I turn my back on you. No longer will I sacrifice, nor will I obey. I am the maker of my own fate.

IX

The sound of voices awoke him.

He recognized the two speaking and peered through the small window. His father and uncle faced each other but with heads hanging and pensive expressions. Tesfahun watched the mumbling pantomime with utmost curiosity. The beads at his wrists and neck left indentations in his skin and they resembled scars to his eyes.

Ogbay appeared weepy and downcast and Kelile gripped his bicep in consolation. He rarely saw his uncle during the daylight. Facing each other, the two seemed of different mothers but in their mannerisms lay the connection. Ogbay's arms hung dead at his sides and he recalled his father's same melancholy posture. Their foreheads matched in profile. Ogbay's mouth lay hidden behind a curly speckled beard and his skin bore early wrinkles given to him by the nights in the sorghum hut. The years of drink now flowed through his blood.

Some clangor of kitchenware startled Tesfahun and he whirled around to find his mother shifting pots on the table. She turned to him a lucent smile then continued her task. He froze, not of fear, but of awe. In the wake of Dunga's passing, he saw a smile uninhibited by her haunts. A warmth came over him.

What are they talking about? he asked, turning out the window.

Something banged and she said, Nothing for us to talk about.

Are they upset with me?

Without looking at him, she shrugged and said, Don't worry about it, Tessie.

The song of her words disappeared. More pots clanged then fell to the earth, one dismantling into thick shards landing on its base.

She stared at the broken pieces without a word for some time before she bent to retrieve the pieces and stumbled, catching herself and shaking like a great wind battled against her.

He scooted off the cot and approached her.

Leaning against the table, she put a hand to her head and began to boil with laughter. The sour breath reminded him of Ogbay. He continued to watch her a moment, balancing against her own senses and bitter blood pulsed through his veins.

Wrapped up in cloth lay his grandfather's sheathed knife. Her laughter interrupted the words she tried to speak as he pushed through the lion skin, erupting into an artificial cackle.

Outside, Kelile and Ogbay continued to talk. He wandered to the side away from the window, facing the tall grass. The effulgent morning sun forced a hand to his eyes as he wandered away from his home. Their conversation and the affairs of his kin faded as he walked away, eager to hear them fade.

When he had come to the young wanza, the tree his mother claimed had sprouted the day he first breathed, he spread his legs and relieved himself onto the trunk. He examined the tree then slowly aimed the stream higher, watching it cascade down the pebbled bark. It was not until he had finished that he realized he could now hear the conversation carried by the soft breeze.

...not after Dunga. I cannot do it anymore.

It is not the time to be weak. Are you not my brother? We own these lands and no one is going to take it from us. No Kangatum roaches, nor the whites with their god.

It's always about war with you?

How can it not be, Ogbay? War is as old as this land. Remember *abat*'s story of the great spirits using blood to feed the plants. It is who we are and who we have always been. I am not a coward.

And I am? I was the one who went to the wilderness that night. I placed him...

Not now. He's inside.

I am an animal, Ogbay's words broke with weeping. We both are.

Stop it, you woman. Why did you come here? To bring your poison to my wife? So she can abandon her responsibilities and get fat and stupid sitting with those fools in the sorghum hut?

Don't judge me as if you are above me, *talaq wändm*.

I have killed but for what is right. For my family. I don't sit around being useless.

A guffaw of disbelief rolled toward Tesfahun, seeming loud in the wake of creation. No words followed and he imagined such fury in the features of his father that he may burst and his uncle will have lived his last. Yet he kept his eyes on the soiled bark.

I prefer you drunk.

Ogbay's words morphed from sorrow to anger, spoken through grit teeth. It was your hands. Not mine.

The voices stopped, silent save the clamor of Wagaye's imbalance behind the walls. Tesfahun unaware he had ceased to breathe while they spoke.

Get off my land.

From the corner of his eye, he saw the round shape of his uncle as he lumbered toward the village. A loud crack came from the other side of the hut, repeating several times before a log flew into the tall grass. Several blackbirds scattered.

Behind him, the lion skin flapped against the walls and Wagaye giggled. The walls muffled the argument. His mother's voice, then his father's shouts. She spoke again then the growl propelled an allegation that it was her fault and a crash erupted from behind those walls.

He flinched, dropping his hands and taking cautious steps backward, feeling the warmth of his own urine under his soles but paying no mind. He charged forward, the sheath dangling from his waist. He slipped through the lion skin and grasped the ivory handle and brandished the trembling blade to his father's back.

Kelile's breaths heaved from his chest, standing over the figure in the corner. The father and son stood ready at interlocked eyes.

Put the knife down, Tessie. You'll cut yourself, Wagaye remarked, her words mumbled by her palm covering her mouth. She gripped the wall and steadied herself upward, smiling as if to show a misunderstanding.

Put that down, *wänd lj*, Kelile spoke soft.

You liar! Tesfahun's voice caromed off the suffocating walls.

I will put this blade in you!

His father's eyes held no confidence in his son's threat but he stepped from Wagaye, shook his head, and fell against the mud wall. His back slid to the floor as if his legs no longer held the strength to hold him.

Seated, he cradled his head into his hands. The ostrich feather forever atop his head, frayed and crooked like some rescinded halo. Tesfahun could not make out tears nor sobs and adrenaline pulsed through his veins. The Great Warrior crumpled in a heap before him and stole the electricity beneath his skin until the blade ceased shaking and dropped to his feet.

Wagaye rushed to him, stumbling like a wounded animal, and gripped him in a cloying hug, kissing his cheeks. She spoke clichéd comforts. Words he heard spoken to Bale.

Her attention turned to Kelile, still holding his head in his hands. She placed pressed into his muscular shoulders, letting her tightly curled, unkempt hair press upon his face. Tesfahun saw nothing he wished to be part of. His mother's gestures so rehearsed, that it seemed a duty she self-assigned. Her role in the village as the crying woman who comforts all of hardship. Alongside the Great Warrior who cannot conquer whatever demons dwell within the shadows of his skull.

He felt the beating of his heart subside only to replace it with hollowness. The longer he stood, the more the scene evolved to an emetic opera as predictable as the rising sun.

Without speaking, he turned and exited through the lion skin, no words of beckon following him. He cared not for the taste of food nor to slake his body of potted water. Even the air seemed tainted and thick with the stolen souls of children snatched before time allowed them to see such a place.

X

He followed the path to Ayana's home. His path interrupted by those who wished to comment on the coming ceremony and assumptions of his parents' pride. He obliged these intrusions with smiles to mask his apathy.

Without prompt, a short, nine-toed man known as Mengesha stopped Tesfahun and spoke of his day as a man, now tarnished with silver hair and brittle bones and broken teeth. He listened with disinterest as he continued, speaking of how he fought alongside Iskinder the Great Warrior during the war with the Muhar and how he had avenged his sister's violation at the hands of those bearded roaches, saving the life of Iskinder when a Muhar had sprung from a tree. His primordial axe descended and he had pierced him with an arrow as he fell. His tale delivered in such an impassioned manner Tesfahun thought he were being preached upon by one of the Kings.

When the man finished, he nodded and spoke his parting and continued as if a legend desperate to preserve his memory.

From a distance, he made out the pyre's ashes. The tenebrous landmark an epitaph to an Akara life. He eyed where Dunga once lay. A circle of mothers sat by the slatted, wanza fence, threading beads upon a string for the ceremony. Their garrulous voices coming to him in symphonic discord like a flock of flittering birds. A few lifted hands to him, shouting words of encouragement and he returned the gesture. He strained an ear to hear what words were spoken after his passing but they had faded in the distance.

He stood outside Ayana's hut and called to her, hearing his own voice resonating with the force of his father and he shrank at his own command.

Ayana's father emerged, rippled with scars and decorated with paint. He glowered at Tesfahun with his lone eye, looking down at this brave child who calls upon his daughter.

Big day soon, boy? he asked with a faint smile.

Yes, sir, he replied. His attention on the closed, flat eyelid.

He chuckled and stepped closer, enough that Tesfahun inhaled a musk, not sour but strong. The aroma conjured images of power.

Soon you will be out chasing down *aboshämane* and cutting their spotted skin for your doorway. Slapping a *gumare* waist high in the river, pulling out those long teeth to stir your soup. Tesfahun the Great Warrior!"

Tesfahun shrugged. I'll start with protecting the cattle.

Ayana's father placed a large hand on his shoulder, hands of a giant rather than the man before him.

It is always good to dream. He smiled. What can I help you with?

The words piled like a rockslide in his throat. I came to see Ayana.

Why?

A simple question derailed his thoughts. His right now seemed so weak since he only had mustered the courage to speak with her once before by the river.

Only to talk.

About what?

Different things.

There are plenty of girls. Why my Ayana?

The air suffocated him. His almond eyes fell vacant. Ayana's father looked down on him with his massive hands upon his jutting hipbones. When evident no answer would be given, he gave a quick shake of his head.

She's not here.

Words still escaped him.

Come by tonight, Great Warrior.

He nodded, open mouthed.

My name is Selam. I know your name.

He smiled, appearing to laugh to himself as his frame disappeared into the hut.

That evening, he lifted the cistern and dumped the water over his scalp. His body startled at the cold as it coated his skin. Dusk cast its orange glow across the valley, ridged by the range and accented by thin clouds against its backdrop. His appetite had left him yet he could not recall whether he had eaten earlier.

He wiped the water from his eyes with a violent swipe and used the fur of a baboon hide to wick away the moisture. He took his kilt and wrapped the trailing linen around his thin waist, tucking the end and smoothed the cloth with the sweep of his hand as he had seen his mother do. Without a cause nor farewell, he left when his mother's back was to him as she shuffled about the cookery, lost in her own heart.

He detoured into the grass, plucking colorful weed flowers and holding them together in a bouquet only a boy could conceive. Short stemmed and dead yellow grass accented the bruised petals. He gently fluffed the plants but they bent wayward. The familiar path to her house felt as if he journeyed the length of the river, over hills and bends. He did not try to ignore the mothers and daughters who cooed as he passed.

Selam waited outside, sharpening a blade as long as his arm. The sound of stone on stone ominous as he approached. A wad lodged in his throat and he swallowed it down and marched on. Selam continued sharpening in slow strokes until Tesfahun stood in front of him. He raised his round eyes and smiled.

I didn't see you there.

He looked around him, searching for something, then asked, It is an Akara custom that the boy's parents come as well.

Tesfahun answered.

My mother is sick and father must take care of her. The words came out monotonous, rehearsed in its dictation.

Selam eyed him and Tesfahun shied at being caught false before the gatekeeper of his affections. He stood, brandishing the blade and watching the shimmer as it reflected the light from the fire.

Come, he gestured, turning his wide chest through the zebra skin.

A mixture of aromas struck him once inside. The children scrambled about as Ayana stood by her mother with a large pot between them. Ayana stirred while her mother sprinkled in pinches and handfuls of dried herbs. She turned and smiled. Her hair cut close and he noticed a new set of beads hung from her neck. Greens, yellows, and reds in succession. Their eyes connected a moment before her mother nudged her arm into motion as she returned to her duties.

One boy with wide set eyes grasped his leg like some frightened primate. Tesfahun smiled and felt the grip tighten. He shook his leg and bursts of laughter came with each jerk. The younger ran up, unsteady on her feet and grabbed the boy from behind. He stuck out a defensive hand, losing his grip and swinging in on his leg before falling. Brother and sister tumbled to the floor. Selam's voice boomed and the children rose, walking as civil as children are capable. The men seated themselves on the floor atop a red and yellow woven rug.

Ayana, come greet your guest, Selam ordered.

She came over and bowed her head. Selam's eyes never left Tesfahun.

Her eyes found his hands and he shot the bouquet forward, dislodging petals and turning the ugly gift into a ragged batch of weed. Her white smile shimmered and she lifted the flowers from his hands. Selam suppressed a laugh at the childish gift.

Is the food ready? Selam asked.

She nodded and returned to her mother's side. Ayana's mother yelled at the two children and they ran in, jumping down onto their rumps. Ayana brought the wooden bowls and seated herself across from Tesfahun. Her mother came last, carrying a basket of crisp flatbread and placing it down in the center before scooping spoonfuls of steaming broth from the stone basin. Her once rope-like lip now taught with a clay plate.

Selam raised his hands and exclaimed in a loud voice, Eat!

Everyone snatched bread and dipped from their steaming bowls. Tesfahun froze, unable to follow the order to the rapacious frenzy. He waited until a pause and struck a fast hand in for flatbread.

The young boy threw a piece of flatbread that hit Tesfahun in the mouth. When he looked up, the boy guffawed, grabbing his mouth. Tesfahun widened his eyes and stuck his pink tongue down his chin and the boy giggled behind his hands.

The mother smacked the child across the dome of his head and he hiccupped through his lips as she gave a serious stare. Tesfahun, noticing the long scars across Selam's chest resurrected the conversation.

You were a stick fighter?

Selam turned his face to Tesfahun, then resumed chewing before answering. How did you know?

Tesfahun pointed to the sporadic scars across his arms, torso, and neck. Selam looked down at them as if he knew not they existed.

Yes, I was a stick fighter. As you can see. He raised his slanted index finger, turning almost at a right angle inward as if addressing the other fingers. My stick dropped and as I reached to get it, he brought it down on my hand. It was Ogbay, actually. When he used to fight.

He looked at the finger, feeling the crooked bone and leathery skin.

That's not all. My right eye, two of my back teeth, and my nose. He pointed in chronological order to each as he spoke them. Ayana's mother kept her attention to her food, shaking her head with each detail of his injuries.

As you can see, I was not very good. He sighed. Not like Dunga.

A brief silence occurred at the mention of his name.

Selam studied his guest.

You could never be a stick fighter, could you?

Tesfahun swallowed some dry bread. Me?

Selam smiled, showing long teeth stained with years.

I just know these things. You could never be a stick fighter.

Tesfahun raised his gaze to Ayana who kept her face toward her food.

I've fought before, he defended.

Whom?

Dawit.

Selam laughed. He would never fight you like a real fighter.

Tesfahun cast his face to his bowl, watching the debris of his broth float according to its own path. Maybe I don't care to fight.

Maybe.

The room grew vacant. Nothing but the rustle of impatient youth. Ayana and Tesfahun would connect their eyes, smile, and then continue with their meal.

When they had finished, Ayana gathered the empty bowls and stood, joining near her mother. The two children scurried off in their new freedom.

Selam flicked the last morsel of his flatbread into his mouth, then leaned his elbow onto his knee, close to Tesfahun. Come outside with me.

Tesfahun nodded, taking his bowl with him as they rose. Selam eyed his hands and smirked and turned toward the doorway. Tesfahun sidled Ayana and handed her the bowl. When she looked into his eyes, relief filled her and they kept their eyes upon each other until the skin covering the door separated them.

The fine dust by the fire pit felt hard and packed on his soles. Selam threw a hacked log onto the fire, spurting sparks upward with a thin crack. He crouched and hovered above the flame like some necromancer as he stoked the flame with an arrow. Tesfahun stood and waited until Selam beckoned him to sit.

You want to tell me something, don't you, Tesfahun?

What do you mean?

Selam sighed. There is more to you than what you let on. I can tell by the way you keep silent. Those who keep silent usually reserve their words because they have important things to say. A man who speaks much speaks little.

I don't have anything to say.

Selam looked at him with an eye catching the flame then stoked the fire again. Tesfahun listened to the crackle of the wood.

Your father and I were once good friends. Did you know that? Selam remarked.

No.

Selam adjusted, now sitting with his knees raised and forearms dangling.

We were inseparable. Almost like brothers. I do not recall a day that we did not speak to one another. And like brothers, we had a natural rivalry. Running, hunting, fighting...women. He usually won but that was fine. I had no interest in victory. When we were your age, we both completed the ceremony and afterward we celebrated, drinking and dancing. That was the last time our friendship existed.

What changed?

Selam shrugged. Your father had a strong devotion to the Kings and their laws. He obeyed and supported them. I, on the other hand, could never align myself with such twisted logic. Praying to spirits, crocodiles, and other nonsense? What good has come of it? Even in famine, they still pray and sacrifice and the skies remain silent. I couldn't live a life of faith. Kelile tried to persuade me but we only argued, sometimes bruising and cutting each other over it. The truth is I cannot find solace in the unseen world. He grew angry with me and has never spoken to me since. But he did not tell the Kings of my beliefs. Which was nice for me. So I took up stick fighting as a means to occupy my time, invest myself in the minds of the others that I believed as they do.

The children fought inside. Tesfahun turned back to the hut but could not see Ayana.

Father never talked about you, Tesfahun informed.

Selam shrugged, I don't doubt it.

Why do you doubt them? The Kings?

Selam's countenance faded to memory and his eyes stared long and deep into the fire and the words he spoke came from long ago.

Curses do not exist, you know. A way in which a tooth grows cannot determine success or failure. Even if The Kings take him and you never see him again.

Selam's features tightened across his face. His fingers wrenched the arrow's shaft.

Yet here we are. Drought laden and famished. On the brink of war. My kin and countless others sacrificed to prevent the very thing we sought to avoid. My wife, she believes what her ancestors thought. I can't be angry with her for it is all she knows. It is all you know. But me, I cannot accept it. I cannot accept killing in the name of drought or vengeance or famine. Killing new life to appease something who is to provide. A god or spirit or whatever that demands such destruction is no god but a blood-thirsty demon. What did he do to deserve such a death? What does a child, a baby, so innocent and helpless, do to be labeled a curse upon his family, his people? How can I believe in a system that preys upon the most helpless of creatures as a target for its problems? They can't fight back or speak or run. Just sons and daughters and brothers and sisters...

He sat, unsure whether to watch the man or be attentive to the fire. The night sky hung black and starry overhead. The village quiet save the distant laughter and shouts from the sorghum hut.

Composed, Selam faced the fire again. His moist cheeks glistened with each subtle movement.

I'm crying like a woman, he remarked, chuckling.

Tesfahun smiled.

Selam stoked the fire once again and wiped a wet hand under his nose.

I've been there, Tesfahun spoke.

He turned his eye to Tesfahun's hunched figure.

Where?

The Valley.

Selam said nothing, but kept steady watch over the flame.

Me and Dawit went. I never told anybody till now.

The children screamed inside in playful terror followed by the reprimand of Ayana and her mother. Selam's stern eyes fixed.

All of us have gone there at some point, as boys but never as fathers.

Wood in the fire popped. I don't know what I believe, Selam. Maybe I don't believe in anything.

Selam set the arrow down and leaned forward, an easy hand upon Tesfahun's shoulder. The warmth of his hand spread through Tesfahun's body.

The two sat by the fire with no more words between them. The night air cooled and Tesfahun glanced back at the hut, seeing the soft figure of Ayana peering in the doorway. He made out her smile in the faint fire glow and he smiled back.

XI

Dawit's home held no faces or sound. No stews simmered over a fire.

Hello, he called as he walked slowly toward the entrance of the hut. Pots and bits of old food littered the ground outside. From the doorway, Dawit emerged. A boy on the cusp of manhood whose eyes bore a consuming vengeance he could not stop. Tesfahun paused.

Where is Bale? Tesfahun asked.

Dawit pointed to a tree in the field. She sits out there now.

Looking out, he saw Bale just as he had the day he heard of Dunga. Rocking below the branches like a broken monument.

She cares more for the dead than the living.

Tesfahun turned at Dawit's words. I'm sorry, *gwadenya*.

What do you want? he asked.

Tesfahun swallowed. Do you think you could help me?

Dawit strained his neck to the side, peering at his mother and hearing the garbled words of his grandmother's loose gums retch. Without a thought, he nodded.

With the hut behind them, Dawit said, Grandmother is going to die soon.

How do you know?

Because that is what people do.

The sun warmed their skins but not Dawit. Tesfahun wondered if he were to touch him his hand may lose its warmth. A group of naked children swarmed past, knocking Dawit to totter with only the need for balance a concern to him. The innocent voices chanted rhymes of youth like a train of a chorus fading. Tesfahun searched the once familiar face that evolved these past days. Searched for a semblance of the Dawit he once knew but found a new creature, one he feared he may never know. Dawit simply maundered, caring not for what Tesfahun had asked of him. Indications of life evident in subtle shrugs and long breaths.

Their wanderings destined them to the river. They took the narrow path to the fields. On the horizon, he could see the cattle with their heads down and tails swinging. Some young men leaned against a shading wanza, bows slung across their backs and quivers full of limestone arrowheads. The cattle lowed when prodded with a spear to move them along. Their rib cages ribbed from their abdomens, curving horns sweeping and cracked. The beasts appeared huge to him and the thought of jumping their backs soon before the village made him keep his distance. The watchmen lifted friendly hands and he lifted back. Dawit raised no such hand.

The path ended at the sorghum fields they were charged with cultivating long ago. The sparse crops jutted from the now arid soil, brown and crisp and as tall as a man. Small birds pecked about the ground and fluttered between stalks, diligent and determined to harvest what little grain remained.

They walked through the crops. Tesfahun pushed the leaves and stems aside with a wave of his hand and the dry plants hit Dawit with no attempt to stop them. The field ended and the shrinking Omo flowed before them. The flat stone still rooted along the embankment, overlooking yellow grass and crooked trees, mountains peaking only to fall like waves closer to the valley. They encircled them, a barrier beyond which lay mysteries they resigned to never experience. Tesfahun ushered Dawit down to sit on their old seat. White marks made by their hands many simple years ago.

Looking out over the river, Tesfahun leaned forward upon his knees. The shade from the wanza tree sheltered them. Across the river, the brittle land of the Kangatum spread into the mountains.

The memories always comfort me here. Like who we were still is playing over there or swimming in the river. I like to think there's something here that cannot be killed, Tesfahun said.

Silence followed. Above, a lizard's scuttle could be heard on the dry bark. He heard Dawit sigh, adjusting his hands next to him, palms down on the stone.

They tell me I'm supposed to kill him.

The flat tone spoke these words, a tincture of abhorrence resonating behind the words.

The Kangatum?

Dawit nodded, never raising his face from his lap.

Are you?

Dawit rocked forward. His bottom lip clenched between teeth before he answered.

Dunga always said he had killed a Kangatum. But I found out later that he was lying. But I believed it anyway. I thought it was better to believe in the belief of someone than in who they really were. My father had told me that once.

Dawit stood and paced slow steps, coming closer to the ledge of the embankment. A curious gaze over the edge. He vacillated his head with the placid river's current.

I thought I would be ready.

Tesfahun watched his friend's subtle movements, evincing what lay captive inside him. He could see Bale in his profile yet carried himself like his father. Shoulder's back and belly distended forward.

You have a choice, Tesfahun answered.

He shook his head. There are no choices in this life. It is better to die than to live without killing.

How can you say that, Dawit?

He turned.

How could I not?

Tesfahun stood, coming closer. *Avenging Dunga will not bring him back.*

But it is what's right.

More blood has done nothing for our people. For us. Killing another Kangatum will only bring more death.

Then tell me, Great Warrior, what do you say I should do?

Don't call me that.

Then he laughed with such humored rancor, Tesfahun felt the blood singing in his veins.

We cannot all be like you, Tes.

What do you mean?

With an outstretched arm, he gripped Tesfahun's bicep and spoke in a softer voice that seemed to quiver.

It is my duty. As a man. Whether my heart speaks otherwise, it is my duty.

Don't become like them.

Dawit smiled again then conceded. *We already are.*

He shook himself free and turned his back. The black eyes of Dawit bore into his skin, their presence like a burn upon his spine. He left his friend behind him. Dawit neither called nor cursed his leaving.

XII

Thirteen cattle had been selected. Donated for the occasion by those still fortunate to have the luxury among their assets. Though cattle by definition, their appearance hovered ever thin to the line of death. Tan and brown and black skin hung from their once engorged bellies, dangling like wet linen from their bowing ribs with every knobby drawl of their feet. Yet they endured. The village bustled as the afternoon sun settled above the western mountains.

Women prepared meals and girls mixed body paint. Bracelets and necklaces and anklets and belts beaded and set for adornment to witness the initiation of the Great Warrior's son. Preparation replaced sorrow and all busied themselves to forget the omens that appeared like warm breath in winter. To forget Dunga.

Tesfahun remained in his home while the village worked. The few times he looked out the window, the constant movement unsettled him and he rocked to battle his nerves. His mother lingered about, exiting and returning with an inauthentic smile. She rubbed his back almost as if her fingers had been replaced by feathers. Between periods of silence, she would whisper how proud she was and he would nod, keeping his eyes on whatever frivolity occupied his attention.

He ate nothing. The drink to come made him nauseous at the thought. In his traditional isolation, his fingers drew thick, muddy works. Infantile in their intricacy coupled with diligence to the minutiae of his imagined scenes. Wagaye peered over his shoulder.

So beautiful. So, so beautiful. I wish I could see the world as you see it, Tessie.

Then she turned, hugging herself as if touched by frost, and fade into herself again. He drew without inhibition, intense to the point his joints ached from the repetition and his hands appeared dipped in a muddle of mute colors. He sighed and looked up from his work.

Where is father? he asked, still focused on his canvas.

A moment and then she answered, He is preparing for your day.

When does this start?

At dusk.

After a time, he stood and stretched his back, jimmying his legs to life. He shifted over to the window and looked to the outer world, hearing faint laughter and songs and the lull of cattle being shepherded into town.

He recalled drams of his childhood of his day where he can call himself a man and stand proud before his people. The countless ceremonies he witnessed played over in his mind. The old desire to one day wear the very feather that rose from his father's scalp no longer fueled him. Instead, as the sun sank, he wished the light would never leave.

I don't understand. Why do I have to be locked away in here?

She shrugged with knees huddled to her chest as she sat on the cot.

Such stupid traditions we have.

She turned her face toward him. The glaze gone from her eyes and displeasure fervent on her brow. He continued to watch the orange-red sun descend before him.

It is foolish. Walking across cows to prove my worth. To make me a man. I should be out there at least. Talking with others, preparing with the people. But I have to follow these rules. I wish I were born elsewhere.

He heard the cot creak. When she stood, her erect posture puzzled him. Her thin lank body glided to him and, with it, her bony fingers. Her palm came down upon his left cheek in a burst of fire. His wide eyes looked to her, a hand upon his cheek and mouth agape.

She heaved and sobbed, two distinct tears slipping from the corners of her eyes.

Never say. There are sacrifices you know nothing about. Do you understand?

For a moment, his body disallowed him to respond, only to hold the composition of himself as she had created. His thoughts raged inside a catatonic body, wishing to lash and strike, speak the words he rehearsed.

She began but her sobs overtook her and she collapsed before him.

As if from a dream, the sound of footsteps came through the lion skin and his father, lathered in white war paint, emerged. His hands brimmed full with bowls of white and red clay, and an empty goblet. Kelile saw his son's face and looked at Wagaye.

It's time. The he turned and left.

Tesfahun stood and followed his father, giving one last glance to the reposeful figure on the cot as the lion skin blocked her from him.

Kelile's long gait led Tesfahun who lagged behind his father's urgent steps. The village resembled an ant's mound. Smiles and waves greeted him from the busy workers. A distant pride on their faces. Old Akara men beamed with fond smirks as if their own flesh had reached this hallowed stage.

Where are we going? he called to his father.

Hurry! Hurry!

Not long after, he saw five young warriors who once fought with Dunga in the arena decorated in white stripes and dots from scalp to sole with intricate patterns unique to each taste. Their faces opaque with white minerals. He knew some of the boys and searched their faces but he knew Dawit was not among them.

Kelile beckoned him to the inner circle of the boys. Ogbay appeared, his eyes burdened but showcasing a smile that unsettled Tesfahun. The group of hands nudged him to a seat and each dipped their fingers into the white and red mixtures. They raised their brushes and used him as a canvas. Their fingers pressed and rolled down his face while each took an arm or leg, belly or chest. Tesfahun's body tensed and he closed his eyes as their hands pressed into his skin and tissue. Their words swirled around him.

The brief bedlam passed and they parted like water from his adorned body. He opened his eyes. The once dark body like some deformed offspring of man and zebra. The patterns disoriented him and he held a silent gratitude he could not see his own face. The ends of the clay began to dry on his skin and gently cracked with every flex. The artists stood around him in admiration of their own hands. Each nodded and smiled.

Kelile stepped closer and said, eyes vibrant with pride.

You look like a man.

With one swift swipe, he snatched Tesfahun's covering from his waist. Naked, he straightened his back, giving the aura of pride. Yet in his belly a fire raged.

Kelile turned to Ogbay. Get the honey and milk. And that is all.

His last words nagged Ogbay and he exited with indignation. He approached his son and placed his arms on his shoulders, pressing his forehead to Tesfahun's.

I know you can do it, *wänd lj*.

He left, heading into the direction of the noise. Tesfahun saw a cow loping in the distance and two black figures in desperate chase. Seeing the beasts come from the fields made the reality of the ceremony even more present in his mind.

The other men spoke to him, offering advice on strategy.

Make sure your first jump is strong.

Only look at the cattle. Ignore the faces or you will slip and fall.

Don't be like Dunga.

They laughed.

He saw that pretty girl and he was only half-way. He nearly pierced his manhood on a horn.

In sweet remembrance, they spoke of Dunga to each other while Tesfahun listened, watching their hard features soften at their fallen comrade.

Someone's presence startled him from behind and he spun around, seeing Ogbay's hairy face. He held a goblet, aromatic with the fragrance of honey and goat's milk.

Is that it? Tesfahun asked.

Ogbay smiled. You'll see.

Kelile returned, droplets of sweat on his brow. Rarely had Tesfahun seen such pride in his father.

They are ready.

Tesfahun looked to his father then Ogbay as all company fell quiet. The crowd's voices were still loud as the group walked past some huts and along a crooked fence until it ended, opening to the area not long ago where Dunga's body smoldered into ash. His presence brought deep booms and rattles from the crowd and a primordial rhythm erupted into the dusk. Groups of women danced, leaping in unison and snaking around the row of jittery cattle. A chorus chanted an old song to the taut drums. Hands clapped and bracelets sizzled.

The man held the cattle side by side while others held fast grips on ropes tied around their necks. Groups of young and old men adorned with paint stood at the head and tail of each cow waiting for the moment.

The beasts lowed and shifted to the music, trying to shake loose. All eyes focused on him.

Clapping.

Dancing.

Jumping.

Chanting.

Wagaye sat close to where he stood, clapping.

Kelile unsheathed his knife and held it high and applause roared from the crowd. Ogbay approached his brother, holding the goblet in reverential hands. Kelile stepped to his son with the knife clenched in hand and lifted Tesfahun's palm.

With the pale skin skyward, he ran the blade along his lifeline as if taking precise care. Red came easily, flowing in a gentle stream through the creases in his hands before falling. Tesfahun did not wince.

Kelile wiped the blade on his kilt then sheathed it, closing Tesfahun's hand as Ogbay held the goblet underneath the clenched fist. Kelile's hands pressed the wound and the stream dripped into the milk and honey. Using a thin stick, Ogbay swirled the elixir. Tesfahun tasted the burning juices of his stomach in his throat.

His uncle handed the goblet to his kin and he smelled the sourness as the thick, pinkish drink, waved in his unsteady hands.

With the beating of drums and chants to exhort him, he raised the cup to his lips and felt the thick drink fill his mouth and slide down his throat. The honey like sap in his gullet. With a grimace, he finished, wiping his mouth and spitting into the dirt.

The crowd hooted and shouted in praise as Kelile raised his hands and called:

The drink shall power him for his path to manhood.

He felt Ogbay's hand slap and sting across his back. The force caused him to lurch forward as he tried to fight the shivers of the foul drink still on his tongue.

Chants again.

Staccato shouts that resembled coughing monkeys that ignited the percussive movement to begin.

The soundtrack moved the earth, sent adrenaline and energy through not only his veins, but the entire village as well.

The women danced more feverish, flailing arms and leaping off stolid legs, diving headfirst into the air to land softly on bare feet.

Ogbay and Kelile escorted him just paces away from the first cow. He looked down the row of bony cattle backs lined with eager faces at each end awaiting his leap. Hands grasped tails and ears. Cows moaned their discomfort against a soundtrack of fire. He did not see the Kings but he knew they were there.

The mass of people blended to one dark backdrop. Their chants turned to white noise. Shrill bird-like hoots penetrated the panasonic circle. The boom of the largest drum in rhythm to his heart.

A cow urinated a broad stream into the dust and another defecated at the foot of one of the men holding its tail and he inched backward and Tesfahun gazed at the man in curious wonder at his disregard. Kelile and Ogbay urged him to begin but he only shifted his feet with each indecisive second. The pressure from the painted faces ever growing in his heart.

He heard a familiar voice penetrate to him through the banal chants and he saw Dawit at the head of the first cow. His strong hands clamped into the neck skin of the beast. A smile upon his face from a time before death had tainted him.

Those mourning eyes looked into him and surged warmth through his skin. His eyes moistened, tears coming that he dammed with utmost urgency.

Dawit beckoned him to go. Do it. Jump.

His father and uncle's voices now joined a familial prodding that stirred within him an obligation to perform his duty. Bestow upon them a pride he believed he had never given.

Bursting forward, his feet ran until his body leapt forward on one foot. His other leg outstretched and reached for the ridged backs of the first cow.

He landed onto the soft skin and rocky bone. Standing on the first cow above the village of spectators, he balanced with his arms swung in wide circles.

Ears rung with the chants, the beat, the swell of applause.

Before him lay the evening redness above the hills as it spread endless across the horizon.

Gathered and ready, he ran. Step after step landed upon the backs. They bellowed and bowed at his weight causing the massive bodies to move.

His foot to slipped. The crowd blurred as he jumped.

Three cattle passed, then five, six, eight.

Exhilaration surged through him like a charge touched by lightning and thunder resonated in his chest. He thought he heard his mother's cheers and though he wanted to not care, something buried within him burned with elation.

He leaped to the ninth cow, his first foot landing into the rib causing the bloated belly to jolt forward. The man holding the tail lost his grip and the animal charged forward, trampling the man at the head, stomping into his belly.

Tesfahun found himself weightless as he neared the final beast. The last hurdle into manhood knocked the air from his lungs as his chest collided into the upper side of the beast.

He flipped, legs tumbling overhead and he gasped but no air filled his lungs. His terrified eyes to the heavens until Kelile lifted him. His breath returned and the terror subsided as his father's rejoice welcomed him home.

It was close, *wänd lj*. But you have become a man.

A defining roar erupted into walls of sound. Voice and song, clapping and yelping. Jubilation in its purest form.

They welcomed him with head rubs, back slaps and embraces. As Kelile draped his arms over his son, he saw two men attend the trampled man. A swarm of lauders came over and blocked the wounded from view but nothing could take attention away from the Great Warrior's son.

He turned back toward the row of cattle that had begun to disperse, now pocked with the bodies of Akara men. Among the bodies, he saw Dawit, across a great divide, clapping his hands. Tesfahun raised a hand and called his name but the words became swallowed in the sea of faces.

The wave carried him away, losing sight of his father and uncle and friend. Strange and familiar faces ushered him on. So compressed among bodies, he traveled with motionless legs.

XIII

Night came and with it the fires.

The frenzied mob transported him until they stopped and dispersed like a burning fog, revealing a vast feast of oryx, milk, bread, and maize. A soup steaming in a stone pot large enough to bathe in. Bowled and cooked, the aromas meshed with the smell of bodies and smoke.

A young girl led him forward to partake first and filled his plate with hearty portions of the rare spread. Once he had received his portion, the others began, snatching food and laughing among themselves. Songs broke out in small groups and the sorghum beer filled all goblets. One brought the cup brimming over to Tesfahun, who recognized the smell and took the cup. In the goblet, he saw his uncle's face and, when eyes were focused elsewhere, he spilled the contents into the dirt behind him for the dogs to lap up.

A new life had emerged from the people. Mired just days ago in the loss of a warrior, they seemed to pour their sorrow into the ceremony. The absence of Bale mute upon everyone's lips, dedicated to happiness and rejoicing and feasting. They surrounded him with faces of admiration as he dipped flatbread into the stew. He had seen a love outward yet he ate alone. The food left a bittersweet residue on his tongue and filled his belly without satisfaction. He searched for Ayan in each girl's face but saw only strangers. He placed the empty bowl beside him and brushed his hands against his thighs.

He hopped to his feet and walked the natural paths of the crowd. Small groups congregated in banter or song. A small, lithe trio of older women danced, springing straight like geysers to the chants of his grandfathers. He wandered among them, all at once a hero and ghost. Jutting above a small group of older men, he saw the ostrich feather and moved, edging his way toward it. His back was to Tesfahun when he followed the older men's eyes and turned, a paternal pride masking his features.

Here he is. My little man! His arms stretched forward, ready for embrace.

Tesfahun hugged him. Over the bulge of his father's shoulder, he saw his mother in the circle, wearing her own mask. Her mouth for him and her eyes for another completely.

You are a man now, Tesfahun. Today, you belong to a mighty people where you will share in the responsibility.

Thank you.

An older man, grey-haired, smile lines deep and cavernous, spoke to him. Praise the spirit for you, young man.

He nodded in return. Looking at his father. His mother appeared in front of him, floating as his attention was consumed and hugged him. He thought to raise his arms in return but they hung like dead vines. A musky, sour odor of her body and breath swirled around his head. She kissed him upon his cheek and he fixed his eyes into hers and his mind kept no order, no reason.

Her voice echoed to him. I am so proud.

Such affection rendered him speechless. He felt the sincerity in their words but recognized the faint shudder within him. His brows furrowed as he looked at his lineage. The mystery of his upbringing lurked the rooms in his mind, clouding the past and rendering his ideals a puzzle without a piece.

Where is Dawit? he barked.

Kelile's prideful mask exchanged for confusion. He gestured to the mass around him in a sweeping move of his hand. This is all for you and you want to know where Dawit is?

He felt a soft hand on his shoulder. We are here. Your family is here, Tessie. Let's enjoy tonight.

A deep eruption rushed from his gut and came to his throat. He turned to her.

Should the past be forgotten?

The older men cast scornful glances.

Do not speak to your mother that way! Kelile commanded.

Tesfahun turned his face on him, standing in the gap between his father and mother.

Or should I be like you? Afraid to stand for what you believe? Selam was right.

The strong hands grabbed the beads at Tesfahun's neck and pulled him closer. The heavy breath heaved from his nostrils like a bull. Wagaye shrieked and put her hands to her lips.

Tesfahun hung by his father's grip, eyes determined yet controlled at his father's rage. The tremble in his hands shocked through the beads and into Tesfahun's chest.

The mass of the crowd faded as Kelile's eyes softened. Concern covered him and his eyes darted across the faces watching. Wagaye's sob song came. Kelile's grip loosened until the two drifted apart. A severance seemed to fill the distance between them.

He kept his eyes affixed on his father as he turned his back. Wagaye reached out and touched her husband but he flung her touch back. The faces stared and Tesfahun, disregarding those around him, walked through the mass of bodies without a glance back. All a bitter song to his ears.

XIV

He did not notice when he had left the crowd behind.

The music and dance resumed faint and forlorn as he maundered near an old hut. The roof patched and no skin across the doorway as stealthy rats scurried past in the night.

He wondered why Ayana had not come or why Dawit did not greet him after the ceremony. Their faces felt lost in the past. Taken by a force he could neither combat or parley. A rompish crash came from within the old home. His heart jumped and he turned to flee until a bloated figure emerged.

Tessie? the familiar voice asked.

Agot?

Ogbay looked down at his hands, holding two goblets full of frothy liquid that spilled as he emerged from the darkness. His belly swayed until he collapsed on a stone in front of the dark hut.

What are you doing here?

Ogbay scratched his beard, then tilted one of the goblets upward. I'm celebrating your manhood, boy. What does it look like I'm doing?

The stench from his uncle's body wafted him back to times where he watched him sit among fellow partakers, loud and raucous. A jagged waving of hands and slurred songs in blasphemous chorus. The smell, the stance, the words all affirmed his existence and appeared as fresh as the day the memories were made. A constancy he both loathed and reveled.

He sat down next to his uncle. The fires from the crowd visible enough to cast an orange glow upon the two through the hut's windows. The color of his uncle's eyes meshed with the fire-glow.

Are you drinking the drink you made me?

He dismissed the remark and shot spittle between his lips that morphed into laughter.

You're funny, nephew. Funny boy. You're like me in that way. Not like your father.

My father means nothing to me.

Ogbay belched and gurgled.

Well, he should.

Tesfahun said nothing, giving his attention to the abandoned festivities. They sat in silence. Ogbay's breath heavy and the chants of the villagers grating his skin.

It's just a mess. I hate it. The whole thing, Ogbay remarked.

Tesfahun pondered the drunken ramblings of his kin.

Is that why you drink?

He paused. A faint reflection came over his eyes and he held the goblet with delicate fingers. The sounds of celebration continued behind them.

That's part of it.

What else?

You don't want to hear it, boy.

I am no boy, Ogbay.

Even intoxicated, Ogbay leaned back, eyes narrowed, and examined this unexpected defiance. His concern melted to humor and he chuckled to himself.

Indeed. You are a big man now. A big, strong man who wants to know everything.

His jocular tone stabbed Tesfahun like sharpened point. Tesfahun's cheeks flashed with heat. Was he not a man now? Didn't the Akara customs give him that much?

Ogbay gave a languid stare as if evaluating some hidden decision he held within him. Tesfahun did not relinquish his challenge and waited. The man he knew as uncle seemed to shrivel before him. Pressed and burdened with such an unbearable weight, the folds of his fat consumed him. The secrets that had defined his life had rendered him limp like a puppet abandoned by its marionette.

What are you not telling me?

Ogbay shook his head and finished his drink in a violent gulp. The liquid swished through his teeth and poured off his chin.

The drums pounded faster and faster. Voices chanting, chanting, melodious chanting. Praise and sacrifice upon their lips.

Your father should be telling you this.

He tossed the goblet and it crashed into the wood slats lining the hut.

But since he is a damn coward, I will do what should have been done. It was always me anyway.

Tell me what?

He leaned closer to Ogbay with curious fervor. The uncle stared at his nephew while a despondent, reluctant countenance burdened those everdrowning eyes.

I have never told anyone this. Not even Bes. Not even when she was sick, understand!

He nodded.

You understand, boy?

Yes, he mouthed, sound coming but from far off.

Ogbay turned forward and exhaled, breathing as if his body could not spare room for his own breath. The music faded from Tesfahun. Life paused for the eve of a truth he suspected all along. His young life always lived among the mysteries of the grown, now one of them, ready to be enlightened to whatever lay ahead of him. Whatever it may bring.

You had a brother.

Sound ceased.

He leaned closer to Tesfahun and placed his weighty arm on his propped knee. The lips lost behind the black, speckled mass of his beard and whispered again.

Do you understand me? The day you were born, you had a brother.

Tesfahun saw in his uncle's eyes a surrender to the poison of a dangerous secret. Though he wished to not believe such a truth, he knew, without a doubt, the key to his existence had unlocked a door he could never return from.

I'm sorry, Ogbay remarked. All will drained from him that even drink could not recover.

Tesfahun shook his head. When the words Ogbay spoke broke through to his understanding, the food, once replete to him, now became noxious. His mouth swelled with saliva while his heart filled with a wrathful sorrow.

You lie. You are a drunk and a liar. Why should I believe you?

Ogbay lent his eyes to the dirt before him.

Go ask him.

The world no longer turned for Tesfahun. Instead, he returned back to the crowd. They danced and sang and ate and he viewed the celebration as a mockery to his life. Between their living bodies, he saw children dance, fleeting glimpses of the cursed. The knowledge ebbed and flowed as he wandered into the crowd and each step sloshed the bitter knowledge inside him. He bounced off moving bodies. A spirit among the corporeal. Drums pounded and voices carried. Flames shot above them all, flicking the night sky. Queer looks and furrowed confusion greeted him until he had led himself unaware past the mass of bodies.

He emerged into the night and his empty legs brought him before the hut of his youth. A lamp burned under that roof of despair. The lion skin hung motionless from the doorway. From the window, Wagaye's shadow appeared. Her combative words responded to the familiar voices until his vicarious self returned, riding the air back into his body and bringing with it the terrible secret of what he had always been. Had he been the harbinger of famine and war? Was Dunga's blood on his hands?

He burst through the lion skin and Kelile turned at the sound, hand upon the hilt of his knife. His eyes narrowed and he snapped, How dare you come back here! You think you are a man now. Find your own home if you wish to embarrass me like that in front the village.

Seeing their faces, he knew within his heart, any semblance of life he once held would forever be altered.

Tell me, Tesfahun whispered.

Tell you what?

Where is my brother?

Their eyes shot wide. What are you talking about?

My brother.

Wagaye trembled and let loose a wail of such haunting it shook the walls of the hut.

Tesfahun, his father began but the words left him.

Where is my brother? he asked, tears forming.

Kelile's eyes dropped and he spoke above a whisper. You know the laws of our people. You know the sacrifice we must make for the sake of the tribe.

Tesfahun stared without a blink. His mind swirled between the living and the dead. Had he passed his brother in the Valley? Did he swim above his brother's bones in the river?

Wagaye's mournful song continued and the same surrender in Ogbay's eyes haunted his father's gaze.

I killed him, Tes. I killed him with my own hands. My own son. I took his life, Kelile confessed in a whisper. Ogbay took him to the river. We had no choice.

Tesfahun looked at the two figures, broken and tortured, seated on the floor of his home. His body floated and he whispered to himself, I am *mingi*.

XV

Sleep became only a word.

The landscape beyond the borders of the Crocodile Man's protection appeared alien to his eyes. Tesfahun could hear the hiss of the river's fury behind him.

He watched the cattle with lazy eyes as they roamed and grazed in scattered groups across the plains. A task he self-appointed beyond the prying eyes of the village. Mouths ground the dead grass and the buzz of flies lingered in his ear. He found an uncomfortable solace at the emptiness around him. The borders of his vision unable to see or unable to care about the life he once knew.

He strolled among the thick bodies and would slap their shoulders without fear of rebuke. Most continued to chew and graze while others paused at his figure.

Eat up, he whispered to them, leaning on his crooked staff.

To the horizon, the bush across the river beckoned the image of Dawit's faceless silhouette on the day he vanished. He had raised a hand but his friend only stared before he disappeared with his spear and vengeance swallowed him.

Across the river, the sun touched the tops of the low mountains, revealing its borders to the unshielded eye. The shadows darkened the clouds that resembled smoke and he recalled Ogbay's pyre from the fields. He wondered if his smoke smelled of beer or nightmares and if his father wept for his brother.

The cattle moaned and he turned back to the sun. To Kangatum land. The mountain people. Where Demissie hunted for blood. He scanned under trees and in bush, perhaps those yellow eyes watched him as he stood alone among the cattle. The Blood Ghost as he had heard him called on his supply trips to the village. He returned to the shelter of the wanza branches after wandering among the cattle.

The sky lingered between night and day. The full face of the moon showed and stars sparked from sleep and hummed an ancient tune. Stick in hand, he hooted at the cattle and prodded them back to Akara land, away from the river. He glanced in the moonlight around him as he herded them for signs of life.

Then he heard.

His steps ceased. Between the clop of hooves, he filtered to hear.

Again. North.

He took several soft steps toward the sound. His mind brought him images of lions, of Kangatum armed with their guns. His grip tightened around the smooth bark of his staff.

Again, it came from the water. He recognized how the sound rippled his skin like a stone in water. The cattle moved onward, further and further from where he listened.

He crept closer.

His blood thickened and suffocated his muscles. Over the edge, he looked down the embankment at the rushing water running along the muddy banks in the moon's glow. He heard the unmistakable cry again and turned north and saw small, orange orbs, three or four a pace apart, maneuvering down the embankment to the water.

He became the night.

Moving with swift feet across the ledge of the embankment toward the sound. The coolness of the air did nothing to settle the warmth inside him. He felt he may burst from within as his pulse thumped within his ears.

From their torches, he recognized the Kings even in the growing dark. Holding their borkotos in their hands. Closer now he could hear their chants. The incantations spoken across the waters and the fire glow caught their mouths as they spoke.

The tallest held a shape in his arms.

Then it cried.

The flailing arms, the legs, the open mouth bearing those two teeth that marked the child for death. From that mouth came a desperate cry, imbued with the terror of the mingi boys and mingi girls at the river's bottom or dried in the Valley.

Tesfahun fell to his knees. The child hung inverted by a fragile leg held in a stony hand. Their raspy voices chilled the air.

Blood ran cold within him.

The embankment had become shallow near the beach, illuminated by the Elders torches. The chanting increased against the child's cries.

Then the tall one's arm reached back and pitched the small figure into the black river. Its body twisted and flipped into the current and the splash erupted through his core, his arms, his legs, and a battle cry came forth with such rage the Elders turned full to face him.

His frame leaped high from the ledge and landed awkward. He collapsed but rose as if unharmed and charged toward those relics and the river behind them. The sharp end of his staff cocked and then thrust forward. One of the Kings cried out, dropping his torch, as Tesfahun collided with one of the towering figures.

The tall King shrieked a loud, gurgled noise, but Tesfahun heard only the gasp of dark water as the river consumed him.

PART II

As the wound inflames the finger, so the thought inflames the mind.

XVI

The current took him south.

His frantic limbs struggled to gain control in the water. Eyes searched but he couldn't find the child.

An abrupt cry came to his left.

His legs kicked against the pressing water and the thought of crocodiles entered him but his mind sought only the sound of the child.

His arms slipped through the water until he felt the soft belly floating face down. Wrapping his arms around the body, the river pulled both into a quick surge of rapids and sucked them under.

The charge of thick water crushed his head and he imagined he heard screams carried in the waves, sunken voices gasping for escape.

His lungs burned like torches until he surfaced and fought against the river with his one grip around the child. The land a ghost. He knew not whether he was east or west, nor if a hippo would rise up and crush him and the child with one great bite. He wanted to pray, but he knew not to whom he would plead.

Under again. A deep sting surged from his knee, resounding in his bone. His mouth released his pain in a flurry of bubbles. Still his arms raised, holding the child as high as his reach allowed.

He surfaced, breathed, surfaced, breathed until his foot slid into the mud and he knew he had reached the embankment. He stammered until the water's grasp slipped to his shoulder, then chest. He brought the child close, nestling the head within his arm. Stumbling as if drunk, he trudged until he collapsed into the soggy banks.

On his knees, he searched against the current, seeing the faint glow of the torches on the opposite bank and a haunting chant riding through the cool night air. Some agony burned through his knee. He cradled it with one free hand, never lessening his grip upon the child.

In coughs he repeated to the still body, I have you. I have you.

The chant increased and he labored up the far bank. His wet feet slick on the grassy mud until he reached level ground. The small hand slapped against his jostling body.

From the ridge, he looked down and saw the small glow of the torches. The moans floated and lulled in his ears and he wondered where his spear had gone. He strained but could not make out their shapes in the deep darkness. But he knew they chanted his name now.

Behind him, the shadow of the land loomed. He turned and saw the low mountains and thick brush and branch covering the ground. He looked back across the river, to the south, hoping to see the fires from the village. Only an empty horizon showed that way. He stroked the child's head.

He stood motionless between the known and unknown. His feet now on forbidden ground and the darkness that lay before him and the boy. The limp hand he tucked tight against his chest.

The chanting continued and he could not bear it. He graced himself one last glimpse across the river, to the wanza and bush and the memory of his past.

The flash of Dawit's silhouette.

Ayana's eyes.

The weeping figure he knew as mother.

The Great Warrior who he no longer knew.

Carrying his load, he turned his back from the river, stepping into the brush with hurried steps and no light to guide him.

He marched through the black, scraping his body on sticks that grew in such a place. They tore as if attempting to rip the body from his arms. But he would not let go.

He bore through, without trepidation for sound, pushing forward and up the gradual incline until he emerged into a clearing. Some half-buried boulders sat in the earth and he stumbled in, limping as the nerves in his knee burst with each step until he collapsed. He wondered if the warmth down his shin resembled blood or water.

First to his knees, then his side. The body still tucked in his arms.

His chest rose and fell with such ferocity he feared his heart may burst.

We're safe, he whispered, holding the child's head close to his lips.

A burden of silence rested on him, supine and exhausted upon the new earth. He gave no thought to what lay out there in the dark. Only the still body he held in his arms.

XVII

The world lay on its side decorated with sporadic geshos and bedenas spreading like hands of worship. He moved his head and felt the muscles of his neck flame. The world absent of the song of birds or buzz of flies He rolled onto his back and raised a swift hand to his brow as light pierced his eyes. The night came to his memory and, after his eyes assimilated to the light, he glanced at his arm. The small body still nestled into his side, close to his heart.

He lifted his torso on his elbows then sat up. The blood in his head sloshed and ran past his temples in pulses.

He looked down at the boy in the morning light. A sliver of white peered through his drooping eyelids. The limbs hung like vines from his forearm. The red gone from those lips. A pale cold he had never felt from human skin. Not even from his father. He saw the white teeth extend from the upper jaw like cursed markers the child knew not it bore. The light showed the child for what he was. His arms squeezed the still body as if he had lost his own.

He raised his eyes and scanned the new land. His voice longed to rise up and yell, to send a plea in the wind enough to burn his throat but nothing came from his dry lips. He dropped his eyes to the body. Flies rummaged about the boy's orifices and, with an angry swipe, he scattered them.

With the body cradled next to his side, he shifted the weight to his legs and collapsed before his feet could find the ground. Front teeth pierced his lip as he grimaced. After a moment, he growled and rose.

On his feet, he could see the river narrow to a stream. He recognized no tree or stone around him.

To the right rose an incline, generous with bedenas and their thorny limbs shadowing the earth. Yellow shapes grew from within, safe and kept. The dry grass extended across the earth like a yellow covering with areas only of dust and stone. He examined the height of the mountain and, gauging the sun, estimated he could reach the other side before the sun reached its highest point. The contents left of his stomach moved inside him and he eyed the yellow fruit dangling among the bedenas.

Pushing through arid air and scratching twigs, he reached up with his free hand, keeping his grip on the child's body, until his hand forced through the punctures and palmed one of the yellow fruits. The skin soft in his fingertips.

He bit into the meat, missing the pit, and absorbed the bitter juices. The fluids rushed from his gums and coated his teeth. He shivered on impulse then spat. Once again, he took a piece, spit the skin, and the fruit fumbled its way down his throat.

With the bitter fruit resting in his gut, he limped toward the mountain. Ache and fire surged with each step of his wounded knee. The ground punished his soles and slowed his pace. This land, so close to his own yet as bitter as its sustenance.

Fear followed him. Subtle rustles and blurred flashes that he assumed were creatures but always conscious of the men of this place. He pondered whether Demissie would kill an Akara. Would his bloodlust know no borders or creeds but only take because it is all he knows? What of Dawit? What if they, in some strange darkness, met one another? Who would kill who? His arm tightened around the body as he pressed through more brush.

The presence behind him did not wane as he pressed upward. The fury and clamor spread through the Akara village taunted his back. The whispers and gossip flicked at his back. The almond eyes of Ayana watched him though he knew this was not so but her eyes stayed with each step. Disappearing into the land he swore he'd never enter.

His tender knee throbbed. He reached out whenever possible, leaning his weight on the thick trunks of the trees. Ants scampered around his knuckles. An army of invisible jaws dug into his skin and he shook his hand free of them. *T'ot'awochi* swung and scurried through the tops of the bedenas, calling, shrieking, as if announcing his presence.

He had wandered half-way up the small mountain before he could not stand any longer. Despite shifting from the weight, the child dragged him closer to the earth. He sat down, pulled by the slope and joining the boulders that rose around him.

Nature's white noise had hovered to a hush. Even the river faded from his ears.

He turned his eyes upward, through the web of branches to the dark bodies of clouds. His skin stuck fast to the cool skin of his burden.

He lowered the flaccid body toward the earth with his burning arms. The vacant eyes and stillness caused his fingers to tighten and, despite his insistence to let go, he raised the body again and rested its lolling head close to his chest. A strange, liquid sound leaked from behind the boy's lips and he loosened, staring deep into those slit, immobile eyes. He shook him, enough so the head lolled from side to side. He repeated this, dwelling on a strange hope of an awakening even the Kings could not initiate.

He continued to climb. The pain no longer sharp but dull, radiating like a dying fire surviving in a breeze. Yet he climbed though he knew not where. Solitude had replaced his fear. A compulsion prodded him to return the child across the river, place it in the hands of the one who birthed him, and mourn together for all they had lost. Yet his hands let the spirit slip through. Hands of good intention now an accomplice to the power of belief.

No. I am not like them. I tried to save him. I tried.

The *t'ot'awochi* hooted from the low branches upward. Small eyes ever watching.

He followed a faint trail, used by tiangs and tracked by leopards, and slipped between scrub brush, using his body to protect the boy. On the other side of the thicket, he could see the peak of the mountain, thin of trees and covered with short grass. Emerging from the shadows, he climbed. He stood erect and surveyed the area from his peak.

Here, he could feel the soft, soothing wind that touched his skin like a thousand feathers and he closed his eyes and inhaled before opening his eyes. To the north, he could see the faint structures of a village. Was it his village? He squinted but could not recognize anything.

In the breeze, his ears believed they heard the timeless and tortured wail of his mother. He listened again but nothing. He yearned for the sound but it never came and deep regret nestled upon him. Even in his retreat, the memory lay just beyond.

Pain surged from his soles upward through his blood and bone as he descended the other side of the mountain.

Memory left on the other side of the river.

XVIII

Shadows crashed and scuttled around him. Hoots and intrigue at this new transient who dared to cross the river.

His mind faced no fear for he knew what they were. Their thick fur and long snouts blurred as they lurked in the bush. Thieves. The color of their curious eyes and bulbous noses revealed their caution and he continued downward without concern.

Halfway, he stopped under a gesho to rest and leaned his head against the bark. His followers paused with him. The brush thickened near the base of the mountain. Each distinct valley met with another hill. The trail he walked from the peak had vanished and become one with the land. No trace of humanity could be found save all that was left of his own.

In his valley, he breathed the air and smelled his greeters as they walked on knuckles at a safe distance. He could not forget their eyes or the rabble of their tongues. With his free hand, he found a stone and gripped it in his fist.

He looked at the boy. The heat caused the body to emit a faint odor and he brushed off the dust and the remnants of leaf and twig from the child's skin. The zip of several flies had begun to arrive during the descent and he fought them as if they sought his own flesh.

He glanced around for shelter and saw none. He licked his lips, feeling the rough peel and wondered should he return to the river.

I can't go back, *tanash wändm*, he whispered to absent ears.

When the pain in his knee waned, he continued on as the sun stood straight above him. He began to ascend another, smaller hill, reveling in the shade of the geshos. Some fruit had fallen and broken open. The smell reminded him of Ogbay and the *tej* that poisoned him until he turned to smoke.

The boy hung lower in his arm and they still followed. One darted in front of him and his stained fangs flashed. Their confidence unnerved him. Tesfahun saw it pause in the bush and he hurled the stone in his fist, missing, and hollered at them. Their callous eyes observed him.

His breath heaved from him in long, fought gasps. He searched the area and, after some effort, he snapped the branch from the trunk. He tested its strength then continued on with the stick brandished in his hand.

When he reached the crest of the small hill, he surveyed and saw more of the same. Peaks and valleys and scrubby brush. He could see no smoke or trails or the remnants of hunters. Only the ravenous followers and the flies that pestered his vision and sought what he carried.

The river had vanished behind him, now immersed within the land. The fire surged through his knee and the soles of his blistered feet. He sat on a gray, speckled boulder, half-buried. With the sky clear of branches, he could see the winged figures circling above him.

The sun made its slow decline toward the hills that lay before him. He looked intent at the landscape for anything but shelter seemed hopeless. His search for water proved just as empty and the bitterness of the gesho or bedena, he feared, were the only options.

His weary eyes looked at the boy, cradled in the nook of his arm.

What was your name?

The blue lips remained and he leaned forward so only their foreheads touched. Neither the cold nor the smell bothered him.

The protest of his gut sloshed inside him, feasting on the few bites of bedena fruit. He went to stand and the fullness of his lethargy came upon him, forcing his body to sit again. A familiar call echoed across the sky. His starving mind repeated in delirious mantra the word 'shelter' as he forced himself forward through pain and drought and descended the mountain, forging a new path.

The surefooted nature of the morning had given way to a precarious balance that, with each step, hovered with the threat of falling. When it came, he had nearly reached the foot of the mountain. He tumbled and rolled while dust flew and the crack and rush of broken twigs sung through the dry air. So famished, he knew not whether he remained in the space between the sky and the earth. Not until his body rolled still onto his belly did he realize that the scrapes lashed across his chest, arms, and cheeks sizzled atop his skin.

Face inches from the dirt, he noticed his arms empty. The last bits of life shocked through him and he sprung to his feet. Frantic eyes searched until he saw the boy twisted around a boulder.

He stepped but then paused. His eyes were not the only upon the child. The male *zinijerowochi* emerged and crept upon his knuckles. The two froze, eyes locked. The others crouched and waited.

The male cocked his head, inquisitive eyes stayed on Tesfahun. Such tension of purpose and desire ran static between them like two runners.

Then the male lunged.

Tesfahun followed and they charged toward the child. Teeth gnashed as they crashed together in a rabid fury unleashed upon this moment in time where both spectrums of nature sought with passionate envy death and its forms.

The male grabbed one arm and pulled, met with force by Tesfahun's hand clutched to the dusty foot of the boy. The old *zinijerowochi* shrieked and hissed and jerked. The same force coiled around the feet, furious and determined as the other. The crowd hooted and screamed in grotesque fascination, cheering their perverse exhortations. He heard but did not see them as if new demons had sprung from the cracks of this new land to baffle into submission all who sought righteousness.

He could feel the bones and joints separate at the force. The male scrambled and hissed with teeth bared in a cloud of dust. With all his strength, his fingers grasped the child's body, desperate to hold on.

Then a blow struck his back and another one had clamored and scratched. The force knocked him down and the child's leg slipped from his fingers. Crying in victory, the old *zinijerowochi* fled with the child and all his troop followed.

No! he screamed as they ran into the bush.

Abandoning his pain and the blood that flowed from his fresh wounds, he followed the rustle and snap of twigs and kept a fervent ear to the crash of the thieves into the bush. Blind to his wounds, he barreled forward with a desperate purpose governing him. The pursuit wove among the stony valleys unknown to him but he maneuvered the trail as if aided by an ethereal force.

Give him! his voice ordered.

They ran into the setting sun and into the night. The brush slapped at him like the fingers of a thousand hands. His mind sought comfort from the hunting trips so long ago. Despite the search for his father's tactics, his memory failed him.

Where are you, *tanash wändm*? he screamed between breaths.

A sound of rustling leaves washed around him as if the arid brush had responded to his cries. He heard their snarls and yips and knew within their hunger would not cease. The gang looked at him, black eyes touched by moonlight. His head swiveled around and caught blurred images.

His eyes could only see the shapes convene upon the body. A black mass neither human nor animal. The horror of their rips and tears filled the night. They feasted upon the child and he sat helpless to their hunger.

Forgive me, he whispered, drowned by the bedlam.

Tesfahun crawled through the dirt into the brush. His knee throbbed and he closed his eyes as he placed his hands over his ears. He rocked on his haunches and hummed through his closed lips. The low, sonorous rattle echoed throughout his frame and he remained this way even after the feast ended and the intruders had wandered off into the night. Hearing only the tortured beat of his own heart, the sorrow of his own blood.

XIX

Weak and laying under the scorch of the sun, he walked through the Valley again. Each cracked twig reverberated the fingers, teeth, and ribs. A wasteland of bones. He smelled the dust like souls of hundreds of his own kind. Now, among nothing of comfort, he wandered seeking a phantom shelter.

Soon, the sun fell beyond where light could reach and the haze of twilight had begun. He knew not how far he had traveled. Where home had been or what food or water felt like.

To his right, he saw a hollowed bush. The last bit of light helped him as he stumbled, first to knee then, as he entered, to his side.

Tesfahun laid his head down and witnessed the first stars through a gap above him. He watched in peace, observing in his faded state the old stars he saw when he sat next to the fire with Kelile's hand upon his back and the land's creation from the Great Spirit's hand.

A jackal whooped among the hills. He studied the stars until sleep came and his tired mind searched to remember those primeval faces so similar to his own that craved child's blood. He heard them linger in the shadows and watched them from behind his covering. If only he had a bow to pierce them one.

He watched the blurred figures prowl on their knuckles in the moonlight with their soft voices so pure, so beckoning, his defenses weakened and he started to stand to let them in. He turned his head and she sat upon her cot with her face turned from him, looking out into the night, and he needed to hold her, feel her there with him even in her sorrow and shame and guilt and those eyes stained by years of torment would not mean what they had once but his legs would not take him to her and her melody of ghosts hummed from her lips that saturated the humid air and outside they prowled again and through the slats of the brush he could see their faces and they were not the faces of this new land but of the old and his heart beat a horrid tempo at the realization of those familiar faces upon apish bodies and he opened his mouth to scream but the sound had been replaced by water and it all gushed from deep within him, running muddy and fast, and the stream would not stop as his mouth became a geyser that puddled at his feet and soon gathered on the floor and rose and rose to knee then waist and higher still and the stream would not cease and the human faces on the baboons were inside the shelter so close he could see Ayana and Selam and Dawit and Dunga and Kelile and Ogbay encroaching upon him till their breath blew upon his face and the stream would not stop and they spoke in a communal voice demanding for a child over and over while their greedy hands grasped after him and he fought them but he could not move quick enough and her melody became louder in his submerged ears and out of the murky black another face appeared and he trembled at the sight and knew the brutish features from the tales passed around fires and the face smiled at him and the fat lips and reptilian eyes came so close they became part of him and he could not scream because of the water that poured from his open mouth, rising and rising into darkness again.

XX

The darkness rattled behind his eyelids yet he could see the faint translucence push of light. His teeth clacked inside his tacky mouth as a harsh jolt shook his eyes open to the slow passing of scraggly brush. The blue above pocked by white clouds that moved along with his body.

Another jolt.

A constant wooden creak tilted his supine head from side to side. He thought he saw hills or mountains, watching as if witness to a stranger's funeral. He tucked his chin and raised his face to see where he had been. The thin path of the valley wound behind him several lengths before the land swallowed the thin line of dirt.

He could hear a low hum of some unknown melody behind him. Shadows flittered over his body.

Another jolt forced his head to bounce and a throb surged through his skull as the pressure of the thick logs and the tickle of the rope upon his skin flared the pain that coursed through his nerves. The hum grew louder yet he could not see and he debated his own reality. The voice foreign and he wondered whether this land had taken him or, if it was Demissie, come to take his life in whatever way would fulfill his blood lust. But he only rode blind and deep by his new guide.

He eclipsed between thought and dream. The river had faded from him. His home too distant to recall. He could feel the shadows from the branches over his chest but no light returned and the shadows became colder until he smelled the darkness. Thoughts of death came to him and he wished to speak his final words toward the Great Spirit but his voice gave only a wheeze that hissed from his throat.

Don't talk now, a low voice ordered.

Tesfahun strained to see his new captor but could not. The yellow light danced upon the dark patches above him. Deep, earthy grooves caught light and flung it across the ceiling.

An obscured figure loomed over him, holding an object in his hand. No face, only voice, and leaned the object closer toward Tesfahun's mouth. His body softened at the spread of liquid upon his lips, teeth, and tongue. Such a small amount slaked his body that his mind no longer accepted death but resisted for the hope. The captor pulled the cup away and Tesfahun raised a pleading finger but a strong, callous hand pushed him down.

Not too much.

The figure placed the cup down and examined Tesfahun's body. He shook his head and tisked. The echo reverberated through Tesfahun's ears.

I'm glad I found you before the *anbäsa*. With all these scrapes, they'd have themselves a good meal.

He could feel the severe pressure of the figure's palms despite their gentle movement across his wounds. The welts and rips scattered across his chest and arms and thighs. Tesfahun tried to see but his eyes blurred and rolled in his sockets. The hands continued to move to his wounded knee and he winced.

This is no good. You stink. It is the only reason you are still alive.

The figure stood and rubbed at his nose.

Tesfahun could smell a pungent smoke that burned his eyes. He longed for more water but his voice failed him. The figure returned, holding half the skull of an oryx like a bowl and stirred its contents with his finger.

He dabbed his tongue with his finger then crouched next to Tesfahun's head. A grip forced open his mouth. Close, he could see a yellow light illuminating the face. A partial portrait which revealed a white, patchy beard and skin and creases that seemed born of the land.

The figure's other hand cupped the skull and then poured the contents into Tesfahun's mouth. The bitter flavor assaulted his being and he made a furious attempt to spit but a hand covered his mouth. His eyes blazed for the first time toward the figure and his partial solemn face said nothing. Despite the hand over his mouth, he swallowed the earthy broth.

A pleased, smile lifted the heavy wrinkles on the visible part of the figure's face and, when he was satisfied, stood and left.

He laid there without time or thought and the surge of pain throughout his body diminished until he could only watch the yellow light dance above him until he faded to sleep again.

XXI

The same hum began deep within his head and mingled among black and dreams until the sound surged and he awoke.

New light flecked across the uneven roof. The steady hum came from behind, out of sight, and the scrape of stone upon stone rung off the walls and into his ears. Pain ignited in his knee but he managed to prop his torso on his elbows. A sweet aroma wafted and his mouth began to salivate with what moisture his body still held.

He faced the entrance with steps down a long, stony corridor where a small patch of sunlight, just strong enough to reach his feet, opened to the outside. His body only allowed his neck subtle movement so he turned his head in both directions, conscious of the low, tone behind him. He pondered his captor's purpose, unable to decide if harm were to befall him or if some noble reason rested in the man's skull. Was he an Akara? Did he follow the Destroyer or belong to those dogs across the river who killed Dunga?

He saw objects leaned against the cave's wall to his left. Makeshift wanza spears, long and knotty, clubs carved from hard, gesho wood, vine nets. Pots. Crude knives and tools fashioned from bones.

The beat in his chest pulsed twice at what uncertain fate may meet him. He rotated his head and saw the cave opened, receding into darkness, and, within the light, he could see a flatbed, tied by hair and resting atop crude, stony wheels. Two wooden handles propped the cart's end upward.

Ahhh, the voice remarked.

He flinched and a shadow from the flame rose behind him and he could hear the soft steps in the fine powder of the cave floor.

He leaned his head back to the figure looming over his body. The man's face displayed a stern, weathered disposition. Deep lines etched under his yellow-hued eyes from the ends of his wide nostrils down past the corners of his mouth.

Paralyzed, he stared helpless as the man scratched his grey scalp with long, yellow nails. The beaded, bony necklaces jingled a melody as his hand sought to relieve whatever pestered him.

Tesfahun only watched the naked outline of the man's face come back to him. He tried to rise and the man crouched down to his head, perched on lithe legs, and placed his big hands on his shoulders.

Not yet, boy.

Who are you? Tesfahun whispered.

The man spat, wiped his mouth with the back of his hand, and stepped while crouched to Tesfahun's side. The fire-light shone over the man's body now and he could see the sunken ribs and bubbled pattern of scars on his leathery arms and chest. The man rested his arms atop his thighs and said:

I am the one who saved you.

Tesfahun grimaced as he tensed to sit up and the man placed a hand behind his back, easing him forward until he sat on his own. The smoke swelled in his nostrils again.

What did you give me?

You were broken so I mixed something to fix it.

But how?

The man's eyes narrowed, wavered, and his back straightened. His eyes evaluated Tesfahun before he answered.

Why do you seek so many answers? Let's get to know each other before I tell you my secrets. For all you know, I could be fattening you up to have a feast.

Tesfahun rubbed his neck. So wh...

Shhh. I'm asking questions now. Who are you?

Tesfahun hesitated at the man's gaze.

Kangatum? Muhar? Who are your people? he asked.

His lips failed to move.

What is your name then since you don't know where you are from.

What?

Did those baboons steal your hearing as well?

Tesfahun paused.

This is my land. I know what goes on here. Also, you smell like baboon shit so be happy I let you into my home. Now, what is your name?

Tesfahun looked to his lap and mumbled, I have no name.

The man clapped his hands, giggling behind his lips. Each clap slapped loud throughout the thick walls. He readjusted his crouch.

Tell me then, no name, what brings you to this side of the Omo?

Feeling the emptiness in his arms, seeing the eyes of the baboons and hearing the tearing of their feast, he turned his face away.

The man's eyes squinted. Are you empty up here? he asked, tapping a finger on his temple.

No reply. The man shot a hand and gripped the boy's cheeks and pulled his face to his.

The man stared hard into Tesfahun's bloodshot eyes until he had made his judgment and resolved, Yes, you are empty.

The boy's cheeks flushed. You don't know me.

I don't need to. Only someone whose head is empty would cross from Akara land into Kangatum without weapons or purpose. This is the land of blood, gägäma. You either take it or give it.

Gägäma?

The man smiled as if receiving a revelation. Yes. That is your new name.

What does it mean?

The man smiled and stood. He walked to the far end of the cave, fingering through the spears and knives against the wall.

I have to go get food, he remarked, picking a crooked, smooth shaft. The crude blade stained a rusty red. He brandished the spear in his gnarled hands and walked past Tesfahun. His joints moved mechanical like a spirit maneuvering from within a weathered avatar.

What is your name? Tesfahun asked to the silhouette as it exited the cave into the daylight. From the opening, he heard the distant voice answer.

Go to sleep and maybe you will fill your head with something.

He strained his eyes toward that light but the brightness made his temples ache. He closed his eyes and watched the white blotches swirl and morph behind his lids. When they opened, he was alone in the cave. Noiseless save the comfort of his beating heart.

XXII

No longer comfort but mourning. Weeping. Ayana, Wagaye, Bale. Their lamentable cries haunted the darkness of his sleep. The sound grasping for him until he awoke, leaving those desperate voices in his memory.

The walls of the cave still loomed over him. Fire crackled near the opening. He heard the familiar tear of skin, followed by the crack of bone.

The old man, hunched with his back to him, worked upon the colobus carcass. The red fur darkened by its blood across a stone table. With his glistening blade, he scored the skin from its body, flinging viscera to griffins who loitered like peddlers at the cave opening. Their massive wings flapped and blew dust into Tesfahun's face.

His aching muscles had healed enough and he lifted his tired body. The blood rushed through his skull.

Do you miss them? the old man asked, flinging a rope of intestine to the scavengers. He did not turn but continued at his task.

What?

I will cut your ears off if they are as useless as you make them to be.

Tesfahun's speech left him. He watched the bony, strong back a moment. He had found comfort in their mourning. His mother's voice always tinged with the ghost of his brother. Since the ceremony, he often pondered if her sorrow was not in the other's death, but in the fact he had lived instead. When his dreams brought her to him, he hated seeing faces floating in the darkness. In the company of the old man, he would have welcomed her sorrow.

It is hard to let go of all you have known, the old man said.

I don't miss them.

You will.

The old man stood, clutching the blade in one hand and the scant colobus meat in the other. The blood dripped from both ends. He walked his rigid walk, tossed the knife with the other weapons, and retrieved a stick shaven at the ends. He shoved one end through the meat until it emerged on the other side then sat with the stick over the fire, humming his foreign tune to himself.

His life now belonged to this odd recluse. Tesfahun rose to his feet, bent in half and fighting the scream surging from his wounded leg. He hobbled over to the fire and eased his way down across from the old man. The griffins flapped and squawked as if demanding more.

The fire spoke between them. The old man focused on the meat as if his eyes willed it to cook. The aroma wafted with the smoke and Tesfahun's appetite returned to him.

How did you catch a colobus? Tesfahun asked.

The old man glanced at him, then turned the skewer. You will have to find out.

The aroma intensified to an almost unbearable desire. Tesfahun stared at the primitive rotisserie, spinning atop the spigot in slow, enticing turns. Saliva flooded his mouth.

The heat warmed him and he wished to shed his skin, allow the air to cleanse his body of its maladies. To open up his belly and let the sweet fragrance fill the cavern of him and satiate his need.

Did your father teach you to hunt? the old man asked.

Yes.

The old man cast a suspicious eye on the boy and Tesfahun shied at the influence of those yellow, hazy orbs. The dirt stuck to his moist legs.

Tell me. Where are your scars? the old man inquired, testing the meat with his callous fingers.

He covered his chest, the finger tips running along smooth contours. No stories to tell like the old Akara men.

I have none.

The old man chuckled. You have scars, boy.

Tesfahun looked at his smooth skin confused. Perhaps loneliness had driven the old man loose in his mind.

I completed the ceremony, Tesfahun justified.

The old man laughed. Jumping over cattle? Yes, you are a man now.

A glare crossed Tesfahun's face but the old man neither looked or acknowledged his rancor.

The old man lifted the skewered carcass and bit from the breast of the colobus. He mangled the meat with the remainder of the teeth afforded him and nodded as he chewed. In one swift gesture, he slid the steaming meat from the stick and held it in his hands, delicate and supple. He ate before the boy without regard. Tesfahun waited for an offer but it never came.

Can I? he asked.

The old man shirked back at the boy's reach.

You kill it, you eat it, gägäma. Thus is the rule of this place.

He watched as the old man devoured the remainder of the food. His barren lips smacked and slaked the juices, the taste, until only remnants straggled from the bones which he gifted to the griffins who waited at the entrance.

The old man stood, belched, and walked toward the back of the cave. Tesfahun crawled after them, pain igniting with each contact his knee made with the earth. The birds hopped and dragged the bones away, never allowing the feeble boy to touch what was rightfully theirs. Tesfahun glared at the old man whose face gave only a lazy, disinterested stare.

When the old man had finished wiping his hands, he walked over and grabbed the boy who had expelled his last bits of energy and dragged him back to his makeshift cot. Tesfahun groaned and winced as his knee bounced and jostled across the earthen floor. The old man laid him on his back and, leaning on his knees, stood over him.

Don't try to be a man. You aren't. Not until you prove yourself one. Jumping over stupid cattle makes you nothing but a fool. Cattle jumping? Only idiots would bother cattle like that. I will teach you what it means to be a man.

XXIII

Wake up, boy, the old man hollered. Spittle dangled on his bottom lip no longer dammed by teeth.

Tesfahun startled awake from mournful dreams. The walls around him moist and crude weapons rested upon the walls. The old man's face hovered above his enough to allow his rancid breath to spread across him. A scowl contorted his features.

You are deaf. How many times must I hit you for you to wake up?

Gathering his bearings, Tesfahun tried to rise again but a dusty foot pushed his chest to the earth.

You have the fever. Do you want to die?

No, he mouthed.

Then lay.

The old man reached over and grasped a wooden bowl, moving it toward Tesfahun's lips as the sides spilled onto his chest.

Here.

He titled the bowl and poured the soupy contents down the boy's gullet. The liquid overflowed and washed over the sides. He struggled for breath but consumed what the old man had given him without question. The bitterness assaulted his buds and he shivered at its potency.

There. And tell me when you have to piss. I'm not cleaning you off anymore, Gägäma.

The old man stood from his crouch and tossed the bowl among the scattered pots and cutlery, piled along the far cavern wall. A thin lizard scampered at the noise.

Am I dying? Tesfahun asked.

The old man spat. I'm no shaman. Sometimes fevers come.

Why does the Great Spirit allow such things?

The old man's cackle caromed off the walls and rattled Tesfahun's ears.

When the old man had wiped his eyes with the back of his hand, he answered, You ask a question with no answer. That is why you are no man. Why did he allow the whites to rape our land? Or the lust for violence to consume our people? The Great Spirit does not answer to us nor I to him. If there is such nonsense.

Tesfahun turned his pounding head to the old man, wild eyed and somber.

I have not killed.

You think it has passed you? You are a fool. We are all fools. There is nothing that governs us but our own evil. It is in our marrow. We created the Great Spirit only to cut off its head and replace it with our own. The Great Spirit is a fable. Created by the elders before the elders. Making us fearful. Weak enough to cast off our own children to rivers or feed them to *anbäsa*. Weak enough to cut down each other.

The old man quivered. He hunched like some grotesque homunculus as if the burden of his philosophy weighed upon him with such force, the very stature of his frame had dwindled.

I am not like them.

He pointed at the boy. The lust will take you. Then you will be just like them.

The old man turned his face and whispered to himself, Just like me.

Tesfahun said nothing.

The old man's black eyes reflected his own image back to him. All that assailed upon him had been his creation. The broth sloshed and roiled within his guts and he clenched handfuls of dusty, barren earth. The granules lodged under his nails, pressing into his palms. He felt afire when the wind feeds it. The walls, the ceiling expanded. A cocoon for rebirth. Shrinking deeper into his cell.

The old man's words buried where his tongue could not find them. The opening closed until no light, despite its fervor, would ever again penetrate. He had the fever and he allowed its passion to burn him, inside and out. A baleful passion that leaked from his very bones and wrapped around muscle and sinew, funneling through vein and capillary until the passion pumped into the caverns of his heart. Beating like the drums of his youth.

We are all formed from spilled blood, the old man remarked.

The fever beset his body and he welcomed its cleansing. He tried to think of his name but he could not recall it. The cursed name of his parents and he grimaced and turned to the pruned face inches from his own.

I am Gägäma.

The toothless smile received his moniker.

Now you are closer to becoming a man.

XXIV

His strength returned and he hunched near the cave's opening, a sentry watch for some unknown intruder. The white light ached on his eyes now grown accustomed to the dark.

The old man tinkered with a broken spear, wrapping a vine around the crude blade. The callouses from his fingertips scratched into the air. The dusty trail led outward, a level ground victim to a steep decline. Dry, thorny bush lined the trail and a rattle of movement hissed among the branches as the wind passed. He surveyed this new landscape as his gentle hand traced the scar formed along the skin of his knee.

The old man muttered as if satisfied and turned. The shaft braced within his hands.

These hands are not so old, see? he said.

Gägäma looked and nodded. Outside, the haze of the sun swayed from above the dust and his heart reveled in the cool of the dark.

It looks hot.

Shut up, the old man snapped and poked Gägäma's back with the dull end between his ribs. He squirmed as the old man prodded him like the very cattle he once lorded over in another time. There seemed a violence in this gesture that sickened him and he sought to flee until the warmth flushed his dry skin and the whiteness of the light imbued him. His hands shielded his eyes as the old man sauntered past.

It's time you earned your stay, he said in passing.

Gägäma followed the tired feet marked by puffs of dust that caught the sunlight. They descended the incline, scraped by brush, and finding momentary relief in the scant shade.

Where are we going?

The old man walked ahead with no response.

The trail curved like an empty riverbed toward the lows of the valley. When his foot set upon that trail, a silence dwelled. The rustle and shrieks of baboons ceased to disturb him and Gägäma stared as if his waking steps had wandered into a surreal vision of the past. A path his bones sung of that lead to old faces and names his mind wished to leave on the other side of the river. The old man continued, impatient and dispassionate to old wounds.

He clicked his tongue and Gägäma followed.

Deeper into the bush, on trails hidden to him, he followed the old man. His mind wandered to the river and the night he plunged into the waters. It was not until the old man turned without warning into the bush into the bush that he returned to the present. Gägäma followed, his body burning with the scratches of the grasping branches.

Before him he saw only the faint glimpse of a foot or a hand before it emerged again. His ears led him. He feared he would be lost until his body bumped into the stolid and ridged back of the old man.

Idiot, look in front of you when you walk, he snapped in a whisper and, two fingers to match his eyes, motioned toward a small clearing blanketed with yellow grass.

He watched the oryx wrap its tongue around a branch and strip the scant vegetation, alone. The twisting spires rose atop its regal head.

Gägäma's heart sunk within him.

Those black eyes, steps away, reflected him back inside himself. To the times he failed in the presence of his father.

Something hit his chin. He licked his lip and felt the taste of blood. The old man thrust the spear at him in an insistent prod.

Gägäma shook his head.

The old man tapped Gägäma's chin again. A soft clack upon the bone. The point inches from his bleeding lip. He took the spear and held the shaft as if he wished to dig a hole below him. A faint image of bones, mounted along the fences, trinkets of demoniacs dangled before his infant eyes.

The animal lifted its great head. Ears perked and still as death. The spear in his hands trembled.

Black and hollow, the oryx eye gazed at his stoic body, half-concealed in the bush. The pupil open and vacuous like water in the night.

A sharp nudge poked his rib.

He raised the spear.

The tip quivered in his hands. Life a horrid adversary he wished not to face, to take as his own.

Breath.

The great head dipped again to the grass. Only the oryx remained in his vision. A flat hand slapped his scalp and the delicate creature bounded with a crash into the wilderness. A tear mingled with a single droplet of sweat and together they fell to the dust at his feet.

The old man gummed his lips as if he had teeth to do so. Violent breaths flared his nostrils. Then the palm came.

The boy held his fiery cheek, eyes to the spear leaned atop the thick brush. Ponderous, the old man stared through him harsher than any words could express then stooped and gathered the spear and continued into the land.

Gägäma followed, his cheek cradled in his smooth hands.

He did his best to keep with the trail forged in front of him. No sign or marker led the way. His only clue the sound of the brush cracking ahead of him.

His thoughts sobbed inside his skull. A mother's mourn he wished to strangle out but the lamentable wail ebbed like a mighty water. Deeper he submerged himself into the trail but, no matter his pace or diligence, the old man's movements faded and he heard nothing but the distant yelps of turacos perched in the wanzas stretched overhead.

He listened. Waited.

A baboon shrieked to the north. The absence of body, of soul, lay hushed within the carapace of the brush. The urge to move filled him but he only stayed, hunched, patient.

The turacos spoke to one another and he often wondered if they spoke actual words and gossiped about the stranger in their land. The residue of the spear's power pressed itself into his hands and he saw the last sight of Dawit's figure across the Valley, the hand raised, his face lost to shadows. The oceanic mourn ebbed again.

The pierce of a whistle penetrated the confines of the bush. His ears perked to the sound but it seemed to come from all around him.

The turacos had begun their dialogue again when the rustle emerged nearby and the old man stepped from the thicket, a monitor carcass dangled like a scarf about his neck. The long reptilian fingers caught upon the coarse hairs of his chest.

A sigh escaped the boy and his shoulders dropped.

I thought you had left me.

The old man said nothing as he brushed past.

He gripped the long, flaccid tail around his neck and whipped the boy's stomach. A muffled laugh as, once again, he returned to his own trail. The boy rubbed the welt and followed, trailing behind with the calls of the turacos.

They made their way toward the narrow path that lay below the valley. Sun and heat sliced through the leaves. The boy watched the lithe tail sway with the steps ahead. The backs of his legs roiled under the skin. A fist clenched around the sinew of his muscle.

When the angled hill rose before him and the old man stomped upward, Gägäma paused. His new sanctuary loomed farther than his eyes could reach. The old man shrunk ahead, his free hand clasped a thorny bush to pull himself. The boy looked to his sides but saw no ends.

His feet found no stone, no station to anchor. Progress stunted with a slip and the scrape of gravel. Inside, he burned. Wherever he grasped, the wounds opened and bled with a lubricant of blood swiped around roots.

He called but the old man did not turn back. Soon, his hands and knees bore into the scattered rock beneath him. The sun scorched all sense of time, of place, and he rolled onto his back, gravel and debris coated across his skin and he exposed his closed eyes to the light.

They returned, shadows behind his eyes. No faces. Only voices. Sound and lament. Each silhouette stood before him, begging account for what he had done. The river child floated before his eyes, a vitreous apparition his eyes followed but could not catch. They called him by name.

I am Gägäma, he spoke back, but they called only his birth name. A ghost's chorus battling to haunt.

I am Gägäma, he said again.

He rolled back to his knees and dizziness swayed against his eyes. But they called and he climbed. Bloody grips on root and stone. Though he slipped, he raised his foot higher, deeper. The clench of his body made his arms tremble.

Higher. More blood. More groans within his body.

They called but he would not answer to their name.

A final push and he fell into the mouth of the cave. The hack of knife on flesh echoed outward. His skin a coat of dust and blood.

The old man paused with his hatchet raised. The kill eviscerated atop a stone table.

He turned and Gägäma caught his eyes before his neck no longer carried the burden of his head.

What in hell took you? Come clean up these guts, the old man ordered.

I am Gägäma, the boy whispered, slithering forward into the coolness of the cave.

The old man shook his head and turned back to his hacking, whistling an ancient tune. His ragged back rolled, contorted with each swing of his cleaver.

The boy reached the shadows and laid with his face mashed to the floor and his breaths signaled by each puff of dust. The knot in his thigh spasmed enough to tremble his leg.

The hatchet crashed across the stone and the old man froze. Blood dripped down the stone like solitary tears, dropping to the dust in delicate puddles.

He turned back to the boy. A savage paint spattered across his torso. The boy's eyes fixed on the old man's shadow that loomed feet from him as he began his story:

My father told me an old tale before my ceremony. Back before houses, before the whites, before war. If that time even existed. A man left his home, all he knew, to prove he was not a coward. To kill the one who had murdered his uncle. The man crossed mountains, rivers, fought with lions and snakes to avenge his family. It took him many days and many wounds, but, he found the one who had killed his family. By night, he crept to the village and rushed at his uncle's killer when he went to piss. In the firelight, he saw the truth. It was a boy. The man held his spear, ready to end the child, but, no matter how strong his sense of duty and honor, he could not strike. So he laid his weapon down and turned his back to the boy.

Gägäma opened his eyes and tilted his head to the man who gazed forlorn out of the cave. The sunlight cast across his chest and warmed his moist body. Gägäma pushed himself up and sat.

He swallowed then asked.

What happened to the man?

The old man gummed his teeth and sighed.

The boy killed him.

With a spat, he returned to his table.

XXV

The old man kindled a fire and, after he prepared the lizard meat, they sat and watched each other across the flame. The old man bit and tore at the chunk of skewered meat, chewing slow and fighting against the sinew. Juice glistened from the white stubble of his chin. The boy sat, shoulders sagging, and watched the old man enjoy his meal. The sweet smell wafted and clouded in the small cavern, taunting, and he savored only his bland saliva.

Unperturbed, the old man cared little to avert his eyes from the boy's longing and relished in the delicate tail, bubbled and black. A leg roasted on the fire. Sharp toenails jutted from the end of the thigh and curled upon themselves until those definitions turned to stumps. His hand trembled to plunge into the fire and grasp the meat, to devour the flesh in one rapacious bite, but his hands could not leave his side. He continued to watch.

I hate *maya*, the old man remarked, spitting some bone.

Can I have some?

No.

The old man took another bite from the cooked carcass and chewed in silence. Gägäma's jaw tensed.

How am I to learn if I have no food?

The old man gestured with his head toward the bowl in front of Gägäma. He looked down at the broth.

This is not food.

The old man tossed the bones at the opening where crows gathered and wrestled for the bones in the waning daylight.

Unless you take the life of your kill, you cannot partake. That is the law.

Whose law?

He pointed a crooked finger to the sunny opening. The boy turned. A crow scraped its beak upon a joint.

How can everything be governed by law? Can't man make his own?

The old man pondered this a moment then swallowed.

Man enacts laws, yes, but he does not create them. The land established laws long before men defiled it. But we ignored those laws and created our own, to allow us free reign of all earth. But our laws will only lead to our own destruction until the land sends its judges to restore what was already made.

So there is no good?

The old man straightened. Man can only do what is right in his own eyes.

The boy looked hard at the ragged figure before him. His eyes black and red, reflective of the fire that danced across his pupils. There sizzled a serenity among the flames and the caw of the bickering crows as if everything aligned as it should.

The old man licked his fingers with an obnoxious smack that reddened the boy's skin.

You still have not told me who you are?

The old man wiped his hand on his covering and stood, turning his scarified back to the boy. He settled in the shadows, knife in hand and a round, wanza branch gripped in the other.

You won't tell me.

You ask too many questions, Gägäma. Why don't you shut up for a while? In the morning, you'll get your chance.

The old man walked past him and the fire toward the opening. The crows did not flinch as he sat among them. Their wings at rest.

He fixed his eyes upon that back and heard the shave of the knife slice thin bark in rhythmic movements. The sun inched further toward its rest and his ancient melody drifted atop the breeze.

He imagined the song carried across the valley, reaching ears both alive and dead, even across rivers where the cattle he once watched paused their graze to absorb the melody of another time. Maybe it traveled further and they would hear it and know, on the other side, his life would be different.

XXVI

A savage poke startled him awake and the old man hovered over his supine body with shriveled lips.

Gägäma shifted his weight onto his elbows and rubbed his eyes. The warmth of the fire had turned to blackened ash. He wished to slip back into dreams but the blunt end of the old man's spear prodded his ribs again.

Stop that! he said.

Get up! the old man echoed.

Gägäma struggled to his feet and the slosh of pain in his head rolled back and forth against his skull. He steadied himself against the cave walls and the fury of the morning birds sung across the dry and arid land. Thin slices of meat hung in long strips from a rack of sticks.

It is so early, Gägäma remarked.

The spear came down across his back. The welt almost instant. Gägäma recoiled and bellowed a moan and the old man shook his head with the spear gripped tight as he walked. He stood at the entrance and surveyed the greyish dawn from their hill, his back arched and erect like a conqueror of a new land.

You want to eat? the old man asked.

Yes.

Then grab that bow. You can't use the spear so we will try something less personal.

Gägäma walked over to the bow and its arrows leaning against the cave wall and snatched them up in a lethargic swipe. By the time he had hung the quiver over his shoulder, the old man had vanished from the cave.

He hustled in awkward strides down the steep grade while the old man walked in soundless steps along the gravelly trail. His body an apparition as it moved through the brush. Gägäma marveled at how silent he moved and both loathed and admired his skill.

They hunted as they did the day before, walking and tracking along the same route and trails, spying the dung piles and faint tracks. Gägäma followed, an anxious rumbling in his gut, and the oryx of yesterday and the ditibag of his childhood stood and stared in blank fearlessness in his mind. He wrapped his fingers around the bow, ducking under the overhang of brush. He licked his dry lips and followed the dusty footprints of the old man.

The cool of the early morning warmed with the rising of the sun. Its rays penetrated through leaves and branches. His healing knee struck against a thick branch and a sharp pang surged. He rubbed the skin as he hobbled back to his stride. The turacos called above them and flitted through the branches. The howl of baboons echoed in the far distance and he bristled at their rancorous call.

They walked for what seemed hours. The rocky hills loomed as they snaked through the valley under cover of brush and Gägäma glanced at their presence against the blue sky. He focused on them and wondered if one day he would reach those peaks and look down on the river and the valleys and admire them, conquer them, but he could only picture the Akara village and the faces he had left behind and the name given at birth he tried to forget. All around, even in the land of his enemies, memory appeared in the minutiae of creation.

He focused on the old man, farther ahead now, and quickened to catch up. The old man disappeared into a thicket and Gägäma snuck through against the violent twigs and thorns that tore through his skin and drew blood. A few paces ahead, the bony frame of the old man stopped. They froze in their positions until Gägäma's muscles burned.

The old man turned his head to the side and gestured with a quick nod. Gägäma approached and came to his side and the old man's intense, yellow eyes indicated an opening where a brown puddle spread. A tiang's long graceful neck leaned forward and drank. The long, pink tongue lapped water from its long snout and the harsh spires rose from its head and appeared crusted with what appeared to be blood.

Gägäma's hand trembled and he looked to the old man who ushered him. Reaching behind, he slipped a crude arrow from its quiver and placed it in his bow. The shaft tapped against the wood as he tried to steady his hand and the tiang's tongue shot back to its mouth and raised its head.

All breath ceased and only the turacos song continued in its natural soundtrack.

In slow, agonizing movements, Gägäma aimed the arrow at the creature as it returned to the water. He drew back, fingers gripped harsh upon the butt of the shaft.

Sweat bubbled through his skin and memory roiled in his chest and gut and he knew he must eat. That this cycle of reciprocity must continue but his soul fought against his body.

He could feel the eyes of the old man urging him to simply let go. The turacos song grew and grew in his ears and the baboons cry in the distance carried the disappointment in his father's face.

The old man's gaze pressed into his side like a spear. The ancient figure said nothing but everything in his intense eyes.

And among the bedlam of voices and the eyes of the land whose thirst cried out, he dug his nails into the shaven wood, breathed, and released.

He did not see the arrow fly. Only the whip of the tiang's head and its back legs buckling before it leapt, hooves raised, and bounded, crashing into the brush and thickets with only the desperation of survival to guide it. The large drops darkened the dust at the puddle's edge and one solitary droplet melted into brownish murk as the violent waves settled.

Gägäma's chest heaved as breath flowed through his lungs once again. A splinter lodged in the nail bed of his index finger stung.

He turned and smiled though he knew not why. The old man gave no expression in those vacant eyes. Gägäma tried to swallow but the parched gums only stuck together when he opened his mouth. The old man leaned on his spear and looked at the puddle, a keen ear listening to the land's direction.

Did you see that? Gägäma asked.

Shut up, the old man snapped and raised a crooked finger to his lips. Then he pointed toward the brush the tiang had plunged itself into.

Gägäma did not speak, but remained silent in his confusion as the adrenaline lessened in his veins and a sadness seeped into his mind. The blood in the puddle had disappeared.

They emerged from their cover and followed the broken twigs and deep hoof prints. After several minutes, they found the body on its side in a puddle. The arrow propped through its muscle and it heaved slow, retched breaths.

Closer, Gägäma could see it was a calf.

Through the heart, Gägäma, the old man said, pointing.

They stood over the animal during its labored last breaths. Black eyes open and pleading. Gägäma stared back at the fading life and the responsibility of those last breaths weighed upon him. The shaft of the bow hung in his palm. His shoulders slung forward with limp arms. The old man unsheathed the crude knife from his waistband and extended it toward Gägäma.

He took the blade and approached the dying animal. He paused, seeing the eyes of *mingi* boys and *mingi* girls reflected in those dark pupils and he leaned over, grabbing hold of the long spires jutting from its head and jerked back. In a swift slide, the life flowed from the open wound and emptied at his feet and those pleading eyes rolled backward and those children disappeared from before Gägäma. The ease of his movements surprised him.

He looked from the blade to the old man with a querulous expression.

Clean it, the old man ordered.

Gägäma stared beyond the blade at his feet now caked with mud and blood. The old man nodded and retrieved his spear from the ground to lean upon. He faced the dead animal and the moist earth squished between his toes. He crouched, holding the blade ready, and stared at the reddish-white underbelly like an unknown territory, unable to fully understand where to begin. Each movement forward caused him to retreat back. The warmth of the day's heat burned his back.

The old man crouched beside him, balancing nimbly with his spear, and pointed his gnarled finger toward the sternum. His voice whispered.

You start here, at the base of the neck, and cut the skin open. Run the blade down the belly until you hit the hip bones.

Gägäma pushed the blade through the hide and sawed at the belly toward the rear of the tiang.

Not too deep, he advised.

Once through the skin, the blade cut easy. The juices spilled at his feet and the body's remaining warmth wafted toward his face.

Now pull, the old man said.

Gägäma reached for the exposed organs and pulled on the slick rope, hand over hand, until its length piled before him. The stench and the flies who had beckoned to death's call buzzed around his head.

Then the old man pointed into the cavern of the torso at the organs and named them as Gägäma pushed his hand into the body and removed each. Some he severed with the knife. The heart he cut out but had to pull with such force the body shifted as if, in death, it would not release itself. When the innards had piled before them and the opportune crows had begun circling overhead, the old man took the heart from Gägäma's hand and tore a chunk from it with his teeth. He chewed the muscle before handing the heart back to Gägäma.

He took the heart and examined the tooth marks in the flesh. The old man swallowed then said, Now it is your turn.

I cannot eat this.

You have no choice.

He raised his face to the old man. Don't we all have a choice?

The old man, beard smothered in blood, looked hard upon his protégé.

There are no choices in life. Only decisions. This animal fought for its life and in its heart lies its essence. So shut up and eat it.

The heart felt heavy in his palm and he lifted it toward his lips and bit. The blood sloshed from an artery and he tasted of the animal's soul. He fought hard against the urge, but he swallowed.

The crows and turacos and baboons discovered their voices once again and cried out into creation as the old man ordered Gägäma to carry the emptied carcass back to the cave. The walk back, Gägäma could not help but notice the tiang's head bobbing back and forth against his side, tongue out and black eyes forever frozen in his direction.

They reached the entrance of the cave near dusk with the horde of scavengers close behind like some morbid procession. The old man ordered him to place the kill atop the stone table and he tossed the carcass over his shoulder and the thud of its empty body bounced against the walls.

With his knife in hand, the old man began skinning the tiang with quick precision. Gägäma watched a moment, sweat sliding down his temples and ache resting in his shoulders.

The old man removed the hide and began to cut into the speckled muscle when he paused and turned his bitter face toward Gägäma.

Build a fire. How else are we going to eat this?

He nodded and gathered the bundles of dry twigs and zebra dung and piled them in the fire pit. He clashed two rocks together until the spark caught the dung and came to life. He blew into the faint ember and it radiated until the twigs ignited, smoke curling upward. He stoked the flames with a half-charred staff and studied the old man's back to him.

He had nearly finished by the time Gägäma's fire raged in healthy flame. The pounds of meat stacked atop the dripping stone table and the fresh hide flung over the old man's shoulder. The remainder of the carcass he ordered Gägäma to take and throw far down the hill for the birds and jackals to partake. He gathered the bloody remnants in his arms and threw the flesh-tattered bones down the hill and the crows cawed and chased the viscera down the slope. Their black bodies frantic against the blood red of the setting horizon.

XXVII

While the old man skewered the choice cuts, Gägäma checked the dried meat hung on racks and showed them to the old man who shook his head and he returned them to their station. The yip and laughter of jackals carried from below the hill but the old man paid no mind.

Darkness consumed the land as it had done since the beginning of time. The light and heat before them flickered about the cave and they sat roasting the day's kill in silence. The sizzle of the fat the only sound.

Gägäma's spirit lingered somewhere between shame and pride. The black eyes as its throat slit open and emptied at his hand haunted his thoughts. The old man sharpened the tips of the arrows with his knife, flicking the shavings into the fire. Gägäma wondered if the very man before him were not some distant portent of what he would become.

When the old man finished the arrows, he checked the heavy meat and saw the earnestness in Gägäma's eyes as he watched it cook.

It is not often we see a kill two days in a row. The emptiness has caused the food to wander further north. There is not much to eat here. Anything else is Kangatum bounty. I think you know what that means.

Gägäma looked to the old man's eyes who reflected fire.

This is their land?

It is my land.

The old man prodded the meat again and Gägäma saw what he had failed to recognize these days in the cave. The sequence of scars banded around his biceps he recalled upon the driver that day in the village. The markings from those across the river and their voracious taste for the Akara blood.

You are Kangatum.

The old man placed the meat on the fire again and gazed into the eyes of this newcomer. A complacent and vacant look that neither accepted nor denied his claim.

The old man's knife rested beside his calloused and dusty feet and Gägäma glanced down at the blade and felt the tension ripple through his body. The old man knew his gaze.

And you are Akara.

Gägäma's heart pounded in the silence.

Are you going to kill me?

The old man laughed a wheezing chuckle and slapped at his lean thigh. His scattered teeth bare and illuminated by the fire.

If I wanted, you would be dead already. He clicked the back of his throat.

Will you turn me in to your people?

Like I said. You are Akara. That is all.

Gägäma watched the old man scratch at his scalp. He inspected the meat, pressing with his fingertips into the thick chunks of cooked flesh. He licked his fingers, and, satisfied, removed the speared kill from the fire. He grasped the knife and Gägäma's back straightened as the old man sliced into the meat and placed the dripping chunk into his mouth. He moaned and savored the moist cut and then leaned forward causing Gägäma to lean back. The skewered meat was inches from his face and the old man jostled the kabob until he reached up and took the skewer.

The old man sat back on his rump and chewed the morsel slow with his few teeth and kept his eyes focused on the flames as if he watched a hidden memory. Where lives past emerged like some spiritual picture show to speak wisdom or caution or something beyond man's grasp.

Despite his weak body, the smell of the meal made his appetite abandon him and he could not turn his eyes from those baleful scars across the fire and how his father had told him that every Kangatum scar bubbled with Akara blood. He bit into the tender meat and felt the hot oil drip down his chin and the flood of taste through his mouth. But his eyes stared over the meal and to those scars and how, in his mourning, he had failed to see.

The old man swallowed and licked the ends of his fingers and reached behind himself and raised a bloated, monkey skin. He gulped the liquid from one of the swollen legs then sighed with the last drop. He handed the skin toward Gägäma.

The old man's eyes, black and fiery in the light, looked hard into the boy's face and leaned upon his jagged knees, patched with ashen skin, and hunched before the fire.

Why do you fear these scars, boy?

I don't fear them.

I will not harbor a liar.

Gägäma dropped his gaze to his meal.

I know what lies behind those scars.

With every scar comes blood. But our scars do not define who we are. Rather, they remind us of what we have been. Of what is real.

Gägäma glanced down at his scarred knee. A mark of failure he wished had never been etched into him. He recalled the bloated body and cringed at the fate he could not change. The fate of his kin so long removed and hidden as if an abhorrence to his own existence.

The soft tears slipped from the corner of his eye and splashed into the dirt at his feet. He braced for the hand that would slap across his cheek but it never came. He looked up and the old man only stared in silence. No pity harbored in those black pupils but an odd compassion welled from deep within a shared understanding.

The old man stood and his lithe frame loomed over Gägäma.

Sometimes the scars we do not see are the ones that haunt us most.

Gägäma wiped his eyes and took a small bite from the skewered meat. When he looked up, the old man had turned and gone to his bed.

XXVIII

The meat lasted several days.

The old man never ventured far from the cave and whittled at the ends of spears and arrows, always diligent to the care of his weapons. Gägäma often stood at the cave's entrance and looked down upon the valley and the arid foliage expanding across the hilly land and would strain his eyes to see as far as they would allow with no intention of spying what he strained for.

They ate, worked, and slept in painful routine and the old man's curt words made life lonesome in a way he had never known in the pastures among the cattle.

Clouds began to blot the blue sky and a cool breeze pushed through the air and across Gägäma's squinting face. All the dead flesh and blood filled their cavern with the stench of putrefaction. Gägäma cleaned the stone table and stored the drying meat in the cool darkness of the cave but the flies found them and crawled across their faces to the point where the old man nor he noticed their presence. When the meat had dried, Gägäma wrapped it in the finished tiang hide to prevent maggots from burrowing into their food.

During the fire, as they sat in their spots and drank black, pulpy coffee from the hollowed tiang's horns, Gägäma asked the old man, When will we hunt again?

The old man sipped his drink. When there is something to hunt.

As a boy, I planted sorghum by the Omo.

The old man sighed. This is not a land of farmers. Water does not nourish this land. It does not understand such an idea.

Gägäma thought a moment.

There is bedena. Plenty of it. If we can find sugar cane, then we can feast.

With a drop of his gaze and a shake of his head, the old man mumbled with an odd authority.

I would rather eat baboon shit.

The fire crackled between them. They had not spoken most the day, despite Gägäma's questions, and the sounds of the night echoed toward the cave. When the old man finished his coffee, he tossed the horn toward the stone table and coughed. He repositioned and stared across the fire at the distracted face of the boy.

You are learning, Gägäma.

Gägäma looked up from his coffee, startled, and swallowed the bitter drink in a quick gulp.

The old man did not smile but turned his head to the side. The rugged profile illustrated the contours of his crooked nose and the lumps of his cheekbones below his eyes.

Always learning, the old man continued. My father was strong. It was said he had carried the carcass of a lion he speared the length of the Omo back to the village in less than a day. Fighting the jackals that stalked him with one hand on his spear. This is his knife.

He held the primal blade in front of him and the black speckled with the fire's reflection. His moist eyes scanned its length in solemn memory and ran his calloused thumb down the blade.

This is a thirsty blade, he commented.

Gägäma listened in silence. The sound of a human voice comforting in his starved ears.

Do you miss him? Gägäma asked.

The old man's forlorn gaze stopped and the stony glaze replaced it. He brought the knife down and tucked it into the waistband of his covering. He stood before the fire, never breaking his face.

He is dead as we all will be someday.

Then he turned and said nothing more for three days.

XXIX

They started in the early morning and hunted the same route but saw no game with which to bring back with them. The dirty water where the tiang and oryx had drank now dried to a scant puddle that not even the turaco cared to cleanse themselves in.

Gägäma feared his luck had run out and, though he had abandoned the gods the Kings had worshiped during his childhood, he could not help but wonder if some malicious residue from the spirit world had finally found him across the river. Perhaps he was cursed.

Since the old man spoke of his father, he had kept reticent, only speaking orders to the boy and keeping those chapped lips closed with a mighty will. The silence nipped at Gägäma and the long gaps between words made his belly ache and hands fidget, ever anxious of a harsh word to reach his ears. He hated himself for such reliance. Yet he performed his commanded tasks with diligent attention and, when finished, he awaited approval from the scowling old man who often grunted.

The hunts lasted longer and Gägäma became nauseous at the smell of monitor and turaco. The dried meat began to dwindle and they expanded their hunting grounds further and further from the river. The burdensome heat made their thirst unbearable.

They returned to the cave empty handed for the seventh day and the old man took the dried meat wrapped in tiang hide and ripped the flank in two. They filled their bellies with some shriveled bedena fallen from trees along the way and the bitterness made their mouths salivate and allowed them to tear the dried meat with their teeth.

Gägäma ate half his bedena and struggled to swallow. With his mouth full of yellow fruit, he asked, We need to find food.

The old man tore some dried meat. I know that.

We could go to the river.

No.

The river will never run dry and the oryx and tiang may have migrated there.

The old man looked past Gägäma at the opening and into the sky, dry and blue as time immemorial.

The rain will come. And with it, the game. Let's just wait.

Gägäma turned and looked at the cloudless sky.

Wait for what? Shouldn't we act and not wait on the gods to save us?

I said nothing of gods.

The gods bring the rain, whether we believe in them or not.

The old man cocked his head and made a clicking sound in his throat.

You are an idiot.

I may be an idiot but at least I will make my own fate.

The old man raised a violent hand and brought it back but Gägäma would not flinch. He kept his stern face toward the old man, hand frozen. A grin spread across the old man's face and he chuckled.

Gägäma's bold eyes softened as the old man lowered his hand. The sound a comfort and insult embodied in one sound.

Why do you laugh?

He took in a breath and gathered himself.

You are an idiot, Gägäma. Finish that disgusting fruit and we will head to the river.

A brief surge of pride filled him, though he knew not what he should be proud of. The old man took a spear and handed it to Gägäma and fetched his own spear with the areas rubbed smooth by his hands. After gathering their provisions, they left the cave.

They headed with the sun behind them and followed the trails made by the beasts that once walked them. Now littered with dry brush and lizards who scattered at their steps.

The river remained a distant memory for him. With each step closer to the water, the ghosts that swam under those currents nagged his mind and crept closer to the forefront from the caverns he had confined them to. He could feel them standing behind his eyes, searching for a means to stand within his vision.

The old man's hunched frame now stood at attention as they passed unfamiliar trails and boulders. The turacos and baboons' voices behind them grew faint. Gägäma quickened and followed close behind his guide. His spear now gripped in both hands.

They stalked through thick briars and their feet smashed rotten bedena as they found brief reprieve passing under the wanzas. The old man stopped and pointed forward with the tip of his spear. Gägäma listened and he heard the familiar sound of rushing water.

They pressed through dense foliage, pushing aside thick leaves so foreign that the sight almost startled them. On the other side of the bush, the old man stepped onto a cliff's edge and fifty feet below the river raged. The rapids crashed with such violent force, the brown water bubbled and roared against the tall, rocky outcroppings.

Gägäma did not recall such a river and wondered where along its fertile path they arrived. Shadows from the ridgeline cast across the opposite rock face. No men save themselves stood near this end of the river. The sounds of the crashing waters assaulted Gägäma's ears and he, at times, feared he heard voices meshed among the collision of sounds. The old man scanned from his vantage point and, several yards down the river's current, he pointed to a pooled area.

If there is no game, there should at least be fish, he shouted.

How will we catch them?

The old man cast an appalled look at the boy.

You are Akara and you do not know how to fish?

They backtracked through the brush and marched parallel to the river until the steepness of the cliffs lessened and a game trail lead down to the water's edge. The slope troubled their steps, but they managed to descend without falling. Gägäma just missed stepping on a coiled adder resting in the shade. A hiss left in the wake of its fleeing.

Giant boulders, slick with wet, lined the edge of the water. The slow current gathered in a deep pool they could access from the rocks and the old man skipped across the glistening, reddish stones in nimble bounds till he reached the water's edge. On the far bank, crocodiles sunned themselves. As still and ancient as stones. A few slipped into the water and disappeared in the murk at their arrival.

Gägäma had clamored on the rocks and, on his knees, reached down to the water and cupped his hands to drink. The old man clicked his throat and reached down for a small stone. He threw the rock and struck Gägäma in the back. He turned a wild eye toward the old man.

Do you want to die? Get away from the water, he said in a harsh whisper. Then he pointed to the opposite bank.

He looked up and then jumped from the water's edge. The half-submerged head of a grown *gumare* buoyed in the center of the pool. Its ears perked towards them, snorting.

The old man, after surveying the area, leaned on his spear and coughed. There is game here at least.

Gägäma looked again at the massive head.

Are we hunting that?

The old man shook his head. Are you going to carry it?

There is meat enough for many days.

He is all fat. And if you want to share *gumare* meat with the *azos*, then jump in.

Then where is the game?

It will come. Otherwise, the *azos* would not be here.

While the old man kept watch, Gägäma filled the monkey hides with water and they found shelter back from the river's edge among an odd formation of stones overhanging from the cliffs. The air cooled and sunlight faded in the narrow passage between the stone walls of the gorge. The rush of distant water and the deep snort of *gumares* resonated around them.

Gägäma gathered some dry brush and sticks growing between the rocks and built a small fire. The small flames enough to warm their huddled bodies. In the dusk, the light flickered high around the stony faces and they watched for glowing eyes in the water. Hands close to their weapons.

The old man rested against a flat area of stone and placed his hands, knife in grasp, across his chest. Gägäma hunched toward the fire and glanced around. The sound of water nagged at him, almost mocked his existence and recalled the night with the Kings at the river and the child he lost. The silence from the old man encouraged his thoughts and, despite the scowl upon his face, Gägäma spoke.

This river reminds me of so much.

The old man shifted his position.

At times, it seems there are voices, weak voices, crying to me from the water but I cannot understand their words.

The old man cleared his throat. They are the dead.

Gägäma paused and stopped stoking the fire.

You know of the dead?

The old man grimaced.

Don't think that you are the only one to suffer, boy. There are always those whose suffering outweighs your own.

Sometimes I wish it was me and not my brother that night.

The old man kept his eyes on the water.

But you survived.

Gägäma looked up at the old man illuminated by flame.

And survival is all we have.

The words agonized inside of him and he saw the bitterness of life in the lines and scars etched into that stolid face. The vocal words an extension of his being and, hearing the syllables vocalized for the first time, he hated the very being for which these words stood.

I don't agree, Gägäma said.

The old man snorted a chuckle.

Does it matter if you believe or not?

Despite the laws made by my people, your people, there is still more given to us than survival.

You know nothing of it, boy.

Gägäma stood and faced the sound of the water. The scant heat from the fire warmed his heels and calves. He imagined the crocodiles watching him with their reflective, yellow eyes, the taste for blood ever present as their prehistoric existence demanded of them.

You think I am a fool because I am young.

No, the old man said, I think you are a fool because you do not see your own nature.

My nature?

Yes, Gägäma. The very nature lying beneath your skin and pulsing through your veins. It is the same nature in the *anbäsa* and the *əbab* who scrapes his belly through the dust. It is what drives the jackals hunt. It is in you now yet you fight it with every breath. And somehow you have avoided the river and the place of children's bones. You do not see it but I do. In every man, it waits and it waits and it waits until the moment when you cannot escape it. No matter how far your feet take you. No matter the cave in which you hide. You will need it and when it comes, there will be no stopping it. In your eyes, I see a thirst and once you've tasted a drop, there will be no turning back. Like a drunk to his drink, it will consume you like the countless generations before.

The old man had stood during his speech and now lingered inches from Gägäma with an intense fire roiled in his eyes. The wrinkled face virulent before him and speaking with such conviction, the old man's lips trembled.

I can stop it.

Ha! It has already begun. Just as every boy from times past. With the hunt. And you have hunted, boy. But it is the ultimate game that we seek though we may choose to believe it is only oryx or tiang we are after. All of us are both hunter and hunted.

They say to seek vengeance but that does not doom me to that cycle.

No, of course not. It is the very nature of your being that dooms you.

You are a crazy man. What do you know about death and loss?

The old man's eyes grew wild in the fire light and his stained teeth bared before Gägäma. He stepped back from the old man and felt the life in his legs ready to send him into the darkness. The old man bit his lips and then spat at Gägäma's feet.

You know nothing, *we'ela!*

Why should I? You do not speak. All this time alone in your cave has made you lose your tongue unless to lecture me or chide me.

Their voices carried across the water, startling the *gumare* in the pool in the darkness beyond the flame. Breaths heaved from the old man's nostrils and his balled fists hung at his side. The stars shone in bright clusters from the gorge's floor. Small illuminations atop the restless ripples of the water. The old man stared toward nothing while a brooding countenance befell him.

You think you know these scars? he growled through his teeth.

Gägäma folded his arms. Tell me.

Why? What would come of such knowledge?

Gägäma waited in patience and stood his ground as the old man turned his weathered back. The long scars stretched down his skin and followed the contours of his bones.

These scars tell you where I come from but they do not tell you who I am. They do not tell you what these hands have done. Scars do not tell the whole story. They do not tell of this knife.

He pulled the blade from his covering with a sickening sound.

Of how far I pushed it through the Muhar warrior who cut the head off my brother. Nor do these scars tell you of the Great War between Iskinder and Bekele, the slaughterer of men. How I spilled life in the bush so much that I emerged caked with dust and blood with this...this blade stuck to my hand. Nor can these scars show you what I have seen. Who these scars have taken from me. What they have taken from me. I was a brother. A father. And now I am the memory in these scars.

The sound of water fell behind them and the old man spoke in sorrowful breaths where memory escaped. Gägäma could not tell if tears came down the old man's cheeks or if he wished to see them. Even the sounds from the creatures of the night had silenced in some unknown moment of solemnity.

The old man held the blade tight around the handle and stared at the stains and notches nicked into it. Ever faint, Gägäma could see the tip quiver in the light. He had no words as he imagined he would and remained with his arms folded, unaware his nails had pierced his biceps and blood flowed through the veins once again.

He spoke a thought he had not intended to verbalize.

Why did you not kill me?

The old man looked to Gägäma, heavy eyes framed by heavy lids and held the knife as he had been.

Damn these words.

He stared a moment and placed the knife back into his covering and returned to his nook under the rock formation. Gägäma stood and absorbed the words and the visions they concocted as he sat by the fire until he laid down and the noise of creation resumed. The image of stars the last picture before his mind slipped to dreams.

XXX

Gägäma awoke as sunlight burned at the tops of the cliffs. The ashen fire had cooled and the bite of a soft wind blew between the rock walls.

He rose to his elbows and saw the old man no longer nestled under his rock formation. His stomach growled and he retrieved his last sliver of jerky wedged within the tiang skin. He glanced across the water and saw no *azos* or *gumares* wade in the pool. Such a powerful silence hovered above the waters.

He ripped pieces of meat with his teeth and stood, stretching his lanky arms and legs. Up and down the gorge there was no sign of the old man and, for a brief moment, he thought he heard the night's conversation echo in the gorge.

From one boulder to the next, he hopped toward the edge of the river. The color no longer a light brown but a reddish dirt swirled inside the waves and he recalled images of the fisherman outside the village trailing their rugged nets across sections of the river. The story of how a long, necked fisherman had spoke of a catfish that had broken through their nets and almost devoured his grown son.

He shook off the dust and surveyed the area. The cliffs towered behind him and lush, green leaves lined the edge and billowed down the rocky sides and the dirt trail made by countless creatures of thirst down the steep incline trickled down to their camp at the base. Looking up at the small gap of sky above him, at the red of the water, life swallowed him in that gorge. Shadows moved against the rock faces and their familiar shapes darted in the corners of his vision.

A shape caught his peripheral and he snapped his head toward the rocks and saw a distant figure. He squinted, expecting the old man to have come from hiding but he did not know the shape watching him from the shoreline.

The figure stood straight without a trace of fear. A long spear clutched in its hand and his dark skin only a trace under the white paint smeared across his body. An apparition of death that seemed born of the shadows of the place.

He moved his hand to his waist but he had left his weapons at the rock formation. The stranger kept his face fixed on Gägäma, sending a shiver of unease through his bones. He searched for any sight of the old man but knew he was alone with this stranger.

A moment passed before Gägäma raised his hand in peace but the stranger would not return the gesture. Footsteps crunched on gravel from behind him and he whirled around, almost stumbling, and saw the bitter face of the old man, whose gaze looked beyond Gägäma at the stranger perched atop the rocks.

Where have you been? Gägäma asked in a growl but the old man would not answer or take his eyes off the figure.

The stranger had moved and placed both his hands upon his spear. A movement so slight as to be nearly untraceable. The feathers behind his shaven head danced in the breeze. The old man gripped his spear and the beads on his wrists gave a succinct rattle.

Locked in this silent standoff, the three waited. The sun had begun to illuminate further down the gorge walls when, without a word or gesture, the stranger turned and hopped atop the slick rocks until his ghost-white body vanished.

Breath returned.

Gägäma's knees buckled enough to cause him to stumble and he leaned over onto his knees and spat. The old man kept his spear raised at the ready with his eyes fixed on the bend. A snort from a nearby hippo broke the calm and the noise of creation, whether it had left or merely been forgotten, returned to Gägäma's ears. He stood up, wiping his mouth and chin.

We've ventured too far. We need to leave, the old man spoke.

Kangatum? I thought you had said we were beyond them?

The old man walked toward the rock formation.

They have moved further. This used to be Muhar land.

Maybe they will ignore us and let us hunt.

If you see a rat near your food, what would you do?

The old man swooped down and gathered the supplies and shoved them into Gägäma's arms then kicked sand and dust into the cold fire.

Before he could feel the weight of such knowledge, the old man had begun the steep climb up the gorge. Gägäma followed. Fear quickened his feet.

They reached the top of the incline and glanced down into the gorge but saw no evidence of their visitor and they plunged into the dark, green foliage, pushing their way along the guide of the river's sound.

Are we returning to the cave?

We cannot go back.

Where are we going?

His heart sunk in his chest but he had no time to feel the loss for they had descended into a new world. Intruders to an unmerciful evil. Gägäma never imagined he would miss the arid land and the bitter bedena.

They snaked through the bush, following the sound of the waters to their right. Branches and thorns sliced their skin and blood dripped from the new wounds and Gägäma wondered if the Kangatum could smell the scent on the lush leaves. He shot nervous glances behind, often believing he saw ghost-white faces in the gaps between the branches or hearing the crashing of rippled bodies through the growth.

They paused to listen for the water and then the old man would lead forward, sometimes veering further right until he could see the river. His hearts pounded and muscles burned but they would not stop. The road did not seem to end until they hit a slow decline and the foliage lessened. As they emerged, the old man halted and pushed Gägäma toward some cover.

Below them, they saw smoke and huddled down among the small bushes, pressing their chests to the ground. Mud huts with grass roofs littered the small valley resting near a quiet section of the Omo. The homes stilted and built high enough to protect them from floods. Women washed down by the shallows of the river's bank and naked children splashed and waded before their mother's beckoned them to return to their side.

The old man surveyed the village and then motioned for Gägäma to follow him. They backtracked closer to the water's edge and saw a pile of huge boulders with gaps large enough for them. The old man sawed some dense brush from its roots and pulled the robust plant to conceal part of the opening. The two backed themselves into their makeshift cave, wedged and tight with only their stench to smell. From their hiding place, Gägäma saw maybe sixty villagers of women, children, and old men.

The old man pointed.

Muhar, he whispered.

Several minutes passed and their breath's shallowed despite the anxiety ravaging their bodies. The Muhar worked at their daily tasks like tiang and oryx grazing and waiting in an ominous calm while eyes watched their everyday movements. Some turacos and weavers fluttered from the brush to their left and the wind from their wings foretold what they had feared.

Gägäma watched the birds dwindle in the distance over the village and, standing off from the nearest huts, there stood a boy staring toward the ridge. A thin stick in his hands. His cocked head curious.

Before Gägäma could speak, the silent horde moved like baleful apparitions down the sloped ridge toward the village floor. A low cry of voices unearthed a malevolence from their souls, bearing spears and knives and hatchets and the power of the white man's weapon.

Short bursts of gunfire rattled and echoed and the women ran in rampant confusion for their children. Old men who have long lost their fight took up their walking sticks in both hands. Scars covered by the sagging of their skin. Screams carried from the floor and into Gägäma's bones and his frantic eyes darted. He told himself to turn away, to cover his ears but, wedged in his place, he had only the option to witness.

The old men armed themselves only to be cut down, ran through by blade or bullet and left to finish their lives in the dirt. The women huddled against their children and took blades through their backs as men gripped the children's fragile arms and shackled them together as mother's screamed and these ghosts, hungry for death, stole their lives before their progeny. Tears welled in Gägäma's eyes and the old man bit into his lower lip till he tasted blood. A small band of Kangatum warriors headed to the river with crying babes swaying by their ankles toward the waters.

Have we brought this on them? Gägäma asked the old man.

We could not have brought what they already carried, he replied. Gägäma detected a tremble in his voice.

The slaughter took moments and the bodies lay as they had fallen. The warriors laughed and took their human souvenirs by knife and hatchet and slung ears and noses and scalps and fingers around their necks and belts. There had been no violation of the women, as Gägäma had heard from the Kangatum, but a lust beyond the physical. A satiation no physical power could fulfill. The children, all boys smeared with the blood of their mothers and grandmothers and aunts and sisters, cried and called for their mothers and fathers as the warriors bound their hands together while several guards watched. Near the middle, the boy Gägäma had seen stood with dust in his tears, hands bound. He saw the boy and such rage filled his body like none he had ever known.

We must stop them.

Don't be stupid. We will just be added to the slaughter. Would you step between a lion and its prey?

A woman, clutching her bleeding belly and crawling from the outskirts of the village, left a dark trail behind her and her groans of pain signaled two warriors enjoying the food left cooking on the fires in black pots. One pointed and the other stood, slipped his bloody knife from his waist and walked toward the wounded. He looked back at the group and they exchanged words they could not understand. He took his time as if approaching a wounded animal he had taken in a hunt. His pale face watched amused as she struggled inch by inch and, a curious posture to his cocked head. He laughed then pinned his foot upon her back, lifted her chin, and slid the blade across her throat to form a new river. A roar of laughter erupted from the band of warriors and they raised their weapons above their head, chanting and singing some melody of demons. Burst of gunfire filled the sky.

They said nothing and holed in their hiding place as the Kangatum walked through the village and gathered sundry items for loot. Others took baskets and placed the bodies of filleted fish along with breads cooked of sorghum and swollen goatskins filled with beer. The line of bound children huddled together among the dead, shivering and weeping.

We cannot leave now. Not in the light. We may have to wait till it is dark, the old man said.

They are evil, Gägäma said.

Akara, Muhar, the whites. It doesn't matter.

Crows and vultures circled overhead, drawn to the fresh scent and examined the feast below them. A jovial song arose from a group of warriors seated on stones among the bodies still face-down. The old man and Gägäma waited in their uncomfortable haven and listened to the sickness of celebration that carried up the ridge. He did not understand the words but somehow knew what they sang of. When Gägäma asked the old man what they sang, the old man shook his head.

Ears were not meant for such things, he replied and shifted his shoulders.

The sharpness of his shoulder blades dug into Gägäma's side. The sun would not sleep and its descent moved so slow and unhurried, Gägäma felt they would die in this crevice as witnesses to their own execution. Fodder for vultures and crows and jackals. The damp air within the crevice cast a somber mood over them. A spider crawled across Gägäma's cheeks but his arms, so confined, could not swipe it away.

So these are your people, Gägäma said.

If they are my people, they are yours as well. Even I have heard of The Destroyer. The one you call Demissie.

Gägäma's eyes narrowed to the young boy still bound and huddled with the others. Tear tracks down his cheeks.

How can that be? I see your scars. They are the same as those murderers down there. So tell me, how can that be?

The old man spat and stared down at the carnage below with glazed eyes ponderous like one lost in a dream.

I thought these visions were behind me. If I had remained how I was. If I had kept the cave mine and mine alone, then this familiar scene would still be in the past with my people where I intended it to stay. But I found you. An Akara. My enemy.

Gägäma's rage flared in his soul.

You should have left me to die then.

I have seen enough death from my fingertips. Why can't these hands be restored?

Gägäma watched the Kangatum warriors drink from goblets and devour the scant food of their victims. Though he tried, he could not see features of man among the ghost-like demons before him.

You were right, old man. This is the work of the place. Either the givers or takers of death. There is no room for any outside of that. I see now. Yes, I see it. I tried to deny it was in me. To justify the hunt as a necessity but I see that death is the only necessity.

The old man shook his head.

Ahhh, you are angry. Anger is good but you do not understand what you are saying. I have seen more of the world and know that one is not defined by where he comes from.

Gägäma stared at the rapacious scene, unflinching as he spoke.

I have seen enough of this world to know no matter how strong we wish to escape, we cannot. Look at you. How long have you lived in that cave? Ages have gone by and still, death like an old friend has returned. It has found you. I ran from the Valley of Bones where my brother was cast away as a curse and look! Look down there at those boys!

The old man kept silent.

When night fell, they pried themselves from the crevice and moved the brush in slow movements. The muscles and joints in their bodies shrieked up and down their limbs like old bones awakened from a lengthy slumber. The fires burned and some warriors began to bother the bound children, slapping their faces as they walked the row of them.

The roots and rocks caused them to stumble through the complicated obstacles of the night. The slice of moon not enough to guide them. With careful steps, they pushed through the bush as if brushing cobwebs from their path. Each crack of a twig or branch stole the breath from their lungs.

Gägäma's head swiveled toward the fires and he squinted hard in the darkness but the children he could not see. They circumvented the village to continue along the river's edge. The old man walked ahead and his figure masked in the thick of the brush. He followed by sound until the fires and the voices faded to only a distant memory. The sound of water soon guided them. A comfort among the howls bellowed through the night sky.

The bloody images flashed behind his eyes with the cries and shrill screams of the dead accompanied those images he could not shake. A wrath accumulated from birth and now he thought of Demissie, not as an animal, but of something larger. Bitterness clung to thoughts of his father and he loathed his diplomacy. A mosquito bit his neck and he slapped his skin hard enough for the old man to stop and turn. Gägäma swiped his hand and felt a droplet of blood, his blood, and he rubbed it between his fingers.

Even after it had dried, he still felt it deep in his fingertips.

XXXI

In the dark, they could not gauge the distance save for the faint sound of the celebration they left behind.

Gägäma's soles ached from the jagged rocks and sharp roots that dug into his heels. They descended a small hill and heard moving water to their right as a cool breeze blew from the water's edge. They stood in the small clearing and caught back their breath. Blood pounded in Gägäma's temples and he hunkered over with his hands on his knees. Even the old man breathed heavy through his nostrils.

Where are we now? Gägäma asked.

I don't know.

They agreed to start a fire and the old man removed his flint from the pouch hung from his waist and sparked the stones together until a dry oryx pellet ignited. The welcome light glowed warm and the old man ordered Gägäma to find a branch to make a torch. The fallen wanza branch burned well and they continued vigilant through the night. Their vision fixed as far as the light would let them see. Strange howls from man or beast echoed from the hills and from the thick tops of trees.

They never strayed far from the water. Something startled and scurried away and the old man swung the torch over but saw nothing. Despite the onslaught of noises, they focused only on the river. They came to another hill and Gägäma feared they may get too close to the sporadic cliffs and fall into the waters from such terrible heights.

As they climbed, the old man said, We need to find shelter.

This is no time to stop.

We cannot keep moving. If we hide, we can rest and set out in the morning. At least we can see our attackers then.

The darkness is our friend. It will help us make our way.

Don't be foolish. Help me find shelter.

Gägäma scowled at the old man's back as they searched for some form of shelter near the river, passing under some trees and down a muddy embankment. Gägäma wondered how people could live in such a place. Walled in and captive. Boulders lined the walls but the old man found none sufficient to his liking.

Not the rocks again, Gägäma remarked.

Tell me your ideas, then? the old man snapped.

Gägäma looked around then pointed around a small bend where low hanging branches carried over the shore from the overhang of rock. The old man followed his finger and then stomped toward where Gägäma had indicated. Their tired feet swept across the slick gravel until the soft, muddy shore accepted their soles.

At the branches, they found a shelter enough for them to sleep and the boulders at the bend concealed them from any who may tread down to the water. The torch had dwindled and the heat from the embers snuck closer and closer to the old man's hands. They sat on their haunches and watched the flame lessen until it burnt out.

I will get wood for another fire, the old man said.

No, Gägäma shouted. Gägäma found his hand clasped around the old man's wrist.

We need to see, he said.

He released his hand and the old man's steps disappeared toward the hill. Gägäma had never known such darkness. His weakened body longed for rest but the anger that simmered inside him allowed no such thing. The images wrestled in his mind. Violent images enacted by his own hands at the throats of those savage men. Something had dislodged inside him and he swallowed it like a bitter drink.

The old man returned carrying a bundle of ragged twigs and sticks. He began positioning flat stones atop the damp ground and piled the kindling. Hunched over and stroke by stroke, he tried to rekindle the fire that had gone out. The humidity caused the sparks to die before they reached the wood but the old man kept at his flint.

It is no use, Gägäma said.

The old man ran the stones together in more fervent motions.

Do you hear me? It is no use. The fire won't start.

It can always start again! the old man shouted.

Gägäma leaned back against the rocks and fiddled with the beads on his bracelet. The old man's constant scrapes echoed in rhythm in their carapace and his disinterest turned to a strange sympathy he had not quite known.

The old man, upon his last strike, fell to his knees and dropped the two pieces of his flint. His chest heaved as the half-moon sliced into the gorge. They sat and listened to the soft sounds of the current. Head down, he stared at the dead fire. A broken mendicant where the moonlight touched him. He sighed.

My curse has caught up with me, Gägäma said.

The old man paused a moment.

Gägäma straightened and leaned forward, disturbing small rocks underneath him and the noise caused the old man to raise his somber face. A serious stare bore through the moonlight.

I am mingi.

The old man's eyes glazed over and he spoke soft, above a whisper as if to speak in such a tone as to not disturb the past.

I had a boy. A handsome boy. You wouldn't know that. I knew he would be strong because I could never catch him and he walked before he could even speak a word. Once, I found him with a deadly snake and he showed no fear. He simply held it and laughed. There was greatness in him. He was my child. But then his teeth arrived...

He turned his face to the river and coughed a trembling hack.
Then he turned back to Gägäma and the moonlight shone off
the tears traveling in rivulets down the mighty creases of his face.

He sniffed and said in a flat voice.

We are all mingi, Gägäma.

Words had no place and Gägäma leaned back and rested his
pounding head against the rocks and listened to the futile cries
of the old man's flint as the river's voice rose in the gorge and
the familiar screams may or may not have been embodied in the
water.

The old man and Gägäma both stared at the abandoned flint
cast upon the damp earth.

XXXII

At first light, they wiped the mist from their skin and left the poor shelter. The growing light afforded them the luxury of seeing where they had come and what lay ahead.

The emptiness of their bellies had stolen the ability to conquer the hills they had descended, forcing the two vagabonds to follow the rocky shoreline of the river. They moved in deliberate steps across the wide and narrow land. The stony wall and the river sometimes coming so close their feet slipped and skimmed across the white-topped water. Gägäma could not keep his eyes from the water and often stole second glances at the belief he saw a child's body face down and riding the contours of the current.

He kept close to the old man and heaviness filled inside his chest as they marched along. He recalled the bloody scene from the previous day and thought of Ayana, gathering water and walking home, and, for the first time since his departure, he wished he were beside her with a steady hand in case the clay pot should totter.

The walls from both shores rose higher, grooved and towering and the loping turns and bends of the river snaked their way through the labyrinth. They stopped and rested. Seated atop boulders, each rubbed his knuckles into their calloused soles. No pools harbored at the edge of their river. So treacherous was the terrain, even the *azos* and *gumares* had abandoned such a place.

This won't end, Gägäma remarked, looking into the brown water.

All things end. It is just a matter of when.

Gägäma stared at the water, looking for but not wanting to find the bloated corpses passing lazy in the current.

Your boy would have been a mighty man.

His caution had left him now and whatever response awaited his intrepid words he cared not to face.

Yes, he would have, the old man replied.

The old man raised his listless eyes and parted his chapped lips that clung together till breath separated them.

We will go on.

Why go on? he asked.

Because there is beauty in the world worth living for, the old man answered and pointed toward the sheer rock face across the river. Gägäma turned and saw the sunlight reflect off a pool illuminating on the dark rocks. A dance of light and song that lifted in the expanse of stone and life seemed worth living if only for that moment.

By midday, they had traveled north several miles and the ache from their journey settled beyond muscle and tissue and into bone. They agreed to navigate one more bend through a narrow stack of boulders just ahead and the old man, now carrying a limp, rounded the corner and hopped down onto the darkened gravel. Gägäma gripped the rock walls and pulled himself up onto the boulder and heard a soft groan ahead of him.

The stony figure stood as if listening. Balanced atop the boulder, Gägäma asked, What do you see?

The old man's frail body staggered right and an arrow showed from his belly. The old man's lazy eyes now full and wild, staring at the rock wall and then up toward the lush greenery that dangled down the steepness of the wall.

Movement possessed Gägäma and he grabbed the falling man before he realized he had landed. He lowered and laid him to his side, careful not to move the arrow. Gasps bellowed from the old man's parched lips. He had never touched the old man before and now he knelt at his side and the skin felt like worn leather. A stroke of wind brushed past him and the second arrow clattered against the stones and Gägäma ran behind a grouping of boulders and crouched.

The river behind him roared. He scanned the ridge above but saw nothing.

Beside the old man, he saw his bow in the rocks. He scanned the arrow's landing and then followed its trail back toward where it came. His intent eyes scoured the horizon and, atop a rocky ridge, he saw the white paint of the scout they met along the river earlier. Markings and scars adorned across his body he would recognize till the end of his days. From his hidden spot, he watched before the scout darted from his spot and slid behind more boulders. The old man groaned and tried to rise but writhed back to the earth.

The scout made another dash toward the old man. His head swiveled as he moved until he found shelter among the rocks. Gägäma tried to focus and remember what the old man had taught him about being hunted and being the hunter. The figure dashed once more and now hid behind rocks just feet from the old man and Gägäma saw the blade in his hand.

He heard the old man's raspy groan and the sound traveled through air and water and tissue and stirred a fire within him he had known existed but denied.

Satisfied, the scout emerged and strolled toward the old man, pausing over the old man's agony with a smirk. Scars held no allegiance for the old man and the Kangatum removed his knife and brandished the crude blade. Gägäma moved in slunk around a crop of boulders toward the two. His feet silent as the grave as the scout knelt down and raised the blade above his head.

Swift like the lion his father had killed, Gägäma burst from behind the boulders and he could see the scars designed along the scout's back and the white chalk and clay smeared across his body. Clutched in his hand, he raised a shapeless stone. At the scout's back, he lifted the stone in both hands and brought it down. The clash of rock upon skull vibrated in his hands.

The scout collapsed as if his bones had melted and landed face down at the feet of the old man. A dark pool poured in between the rocks.

Gägäma felt the echo of the vibration carom back from its furthermost regions and channeled through his trembling hands. The stone, spattered with patches of deep red, came down on the fallen man again and again with no relent. Into his hands, he poured anger and sorrow and loss and witness until the crack of rock upon bone turned to the clatter of stone upon stone. A solitary metronome beating the gaps from generations.

He paused as he raised for another strike but saw nothing remained of the Kangatum skull and he dropped the weapon back to the earth, wiping the sweat from his face. But when he removed his hand, he saw only a palm soaked in red. He wiped again with both his hands and they came away the same. He had imagined what he would feel should this day ever come and how he would vomit and cry for what he had done. But he realized dreams mean nothing and a life lived in what could be is not life for he felt nothing.

The old man tried to move again but cried out as the arrow moved in his tissue. Gägäma came to his side and tried to raise him. The rocks underneath slippery and dark. The old man's head lolled as if unable to carry the weight of the pain and the whites of his tired eyes rolled toward the sky. His trembling hands patted the old man's shoulder and he knew he should move or take care, but he remained paralyzed.

You'll be alright, he assured.

The old man blinked hard in response and gasped. Breath wheezed from his lips and blood bubbled around the arrow shaft. One hand gripped around the shaft in his stomach and the other wrapped tight around Gägäma's forearm.

I-I will take it out. Hold still, he said and grabbed the shaft close to the skin. The slightest pull triggered a seizure of movement and the hand around his arm flung and slapped Gägäma across the face.

We have to take it out, he insisted.

The old man raised his head up and wheezed, No. Leave it.

In one quick breath, he dropped his head to rest on the rocks and dirt.

Please. L-Let me. Please, he whispered but the old man lifted his hand toward Gägäma and, with a weak grip, took the boy's bloody hands and guided it toward the covering in his belt. The handle of the knife pressed into Gägäma's palm and he shook his head. Droplets of sweat dripped from his chin.

No. You won't die now. Just let me help you, he said.

The old man placed his rough palm atop his hand and pushed the fingers so they closed around the handle. Gägäma dropped his gaze to the rocks. The weak hand lifted his and the knife slipped from the belt and they raised the knife together, hand upon hand, until the knife, blade down, hovered above the old man's heart.

Gägäma looked up through blurred eyes and shook his head. I can't. I can't do it.

The old man shook and caused the blade to waver but held the knife aloft. He turned his eyes and looked deep into the soul of the one he had saved and Gägäma knew nothing would be the same.

He choked on the guilt in his throat and whispered, I'm sorry you saved me, *astämari*.

The old man released his other hand from the arrow and raised himself up and reached out and wrapped his hand around Gägäma's neck and pulled himself close so Gägäma could smell the faint malodor of death approaching. He placed his forehead against Gägäma's own and his touch imparted a comfort that spread from skin to skin and, with a long breath reserved, said, No, *wänd lj*, you have saved me. This is your blade now.

With a last lunge of strength, the old man pulled his face past Gägäma's shoulder and pushed down the hand he held, plunging the crude blade through flesh and bone with such force it stole the very breath from him. Gägäma could not move nor protest and held the old man as he shivered the remainder of his life away and he clutched the body he had never embraced and sobbed harder than he knew existed.

Under the sun and beside the waters, he knelt among two bodies of which he knew neither name and cried out to creation and the past in such lament he cared not who heard nor who came. He cared not for the pain the small stones caused in his knees or the blood sticky on his hands. He wept for all he had lost for it was only in loss he had solace. One hand on the knife and the other around the old man's body. Each covered in blood not his own but mirrored in color and texture as the coldness of shadows fell across him once more, between walls so high, he could not see a way over.

XXXIII

He left the bodies and the rocks that slaked their blood behind and walked the path the old man had started.

The river flowed to his right in the rocky gorge and he cared not for the slender monsters and their yellow eyes sun bathing on the soft, muddy banks. Some turned their bodies in whip-like fashion and disappeared into the brown water as he passed. The blood once fresh on his face now dried and caked against his skin save for the trails carved by his tears.

His tired bones led him down a foreign path of unknown brush and landmarks he had never imagined. Hidden posts brimmed with the possibility of some predator yet he walked on with a tired abandon. A tight fist clenched around the bloody knife.

The reality of the Kangatum tracking him lingered in his mind and the life of the scout upon him, he knew they would come for him. But the images of their slaughter resonated no fear for, in their ghost-white faces and decorated scars, he saw jackals and dogs who stole upon the defeated and claimed it as victory. He saw their mongrel faces and the bodies of Dunga and Dawit gnawed upon by their inhuman fangs. These visions brewed inside him and he wandered further from the cave and the Muhar village and the old man deeper into the waning sunlight until he was consumed within the heart of darkness.

He dropped to his knees wherever they gave out on him and he gathered the sparse dry weeds that grew along the shore and bundled them among a circle of stones. Using the old man's flint he had taken with him, he lit the fire as he learned in three strikes. The light caught the eyes of the *azos* reflected atop the calm water.

Such loneliness overtook him yet the presence of the old man still brought comfort among all those fires. He looked above the rocky walls at the bluish black sky and the myriad of stars above him. His mother's voice spoke faint from the past and gradually grew and grew until he remembered her arms wrapped around him by the edge of the village and both their eyes fixed on the sky and she told him a story of generations about the dead's spirits encapsulated in those lights that always watched over them. All creation side by side with the gods who sanctioned their dwellings.

Her voice would not leave him and he knew Tesfahun would never return. Nor was he Gägäma. No longer a boy but a man of the Omo and an understanding settled on him. Maybe isolation afforded him the opportunity to listen. To hear for the first time. To see with the eyes he had forcibly blinded.

He stood from the fire and walked to the calm river's edge and the yellow eyes that disappeared under the water. In a deep breath, he removed his new blade from his belt and held it high in the fire light. And, under the stars of all those above him, he declared himself nameless to the world but, instead, as a new creature from the violence creation had required of him. The incomprehensible war-cry rattled from his throat and strained out until it shattered the stillness and bent to his will. He hoped the sound reached the stars and deafened the spirits.

His fists shook in a clumsy tremble and his chest heaved looking across dark waters and the dry, tacky blood broke when he smiled. He relished the new breaths and his lips mumbled vengeance for the first time and he thought he tasted the flecks of blood from his face. The flavor lingered on his tongue.

He turned back to the fire and his once tired and hopeless legs sprung to life and he stepped across the uneven gravel. When his eyes focused at the fire ahead, he stopped.

A ghost watched him and held the weapon of the white man and, in the other hand, a blade made of earth and bone. Even in the darkness, the ripple of his massive arms and the spattering of scars painted across his entire body penetrated like the stars above.

As the flames rose, his head seemed to stay above the fire. Was this beast Kangatum? Muhar? No matter. He knew death had come for him.

PART III

It is foolish to start a fire just to see the flames.

XXXIV

The two stood with the fire between them.

Only the river's steady flow filled the gorge. The immense figure visible in the light and the long barrel of his metal weapon high above his head that resembled the ostrich feather his father wore.

The man waited.

This is no place for a boy, the man remarked.

He straightened his back and held his chin high, a hard grip around the old man's blade.

I am no longer a boy.

An amused smirk spread on the man's lips and he folded his swollen arms across his chest. Eyes scanned the boy's body as if he found the sight before him a player in a comedy.

Blood pulsed through his body and his new hatred fueled him. His stance ready and defiant.

You call yourself a man and you use the white man's weapon.

The man paused, a quizzical look on his grotesque features. You remind me of someone.

Silent, the boy shifted his grip on the old man's knife.

Recognition softened the man's face and he nodded to himself. You are Akara.

And you are Kangatum filth.

The man stepped over the fire in one stride, perhaps into it, and lumbered toward him with a strong swagger. Bracing backward, the boy fought the urge to dive into the river and let the crocodiles take him but he stood his ground as the true power of this stranger revealed itself just steps from him. The crude scars resembled scales and covered his body in new skin. Across his chest, he saw a familiar pattern of scars decorated just like his father.

You know my name, the man spoke.

The faceless one had now been seen and the nightmares shared among his people now towered above him and he wondered if the legend or the reality carried more terror.

Demissie, the boy whispered.

Out here, little warrior, we are all the same.

As the boy trembled before him, Demissie examined his unmarked skin.

Do you know war? He asked.

The boy's tongue refused to move and, though he wished to speak, he only wavered in the presence of The Destroyer.

War is an evolution. And if you do not evolve, death will find new ways to take you unless you combat it with its own means. And when death comes for you as it comes for me, I will be ready.

Demissie's eyes reflected no light from the fire.

So I ask you, why are you here?

He kept his gaze at the scarified face and fought the urge to look away but he knew that time had ended. Those perilous orbs and primitive nose and slaking lips held no fear as they once had. He stood and spoke.

To join you.

Demissie sighed deeply through his nose.

Yes?

The boy nodded.

Then take that blade and shove it in my heart.

His knuckles gripped around the blade. His pulse thundered like the waters behind him. He saw the life fade from the old man once again. The light shivered from his yellow-hued eyes and a spark ignited within his bones.

Before him stood the symbol of death and in that figure, he directed his malice and pain. His arm lunged forward and the back of Demissie's massive hand deflected his strike and threw him on the rocks, landing inches from the fading fire. The pain stung in his knees but he sprung to his feet, hunched with arms out and teeth bared. Demissie followed his movements with his eyes only, sauntering to his left with the flame.

Come. Take your revenge. Like your father did.

The boy screamed and charged, missing as a heavy blow from Demissie's elbow crashed atop his spine, sending him back to the rocks.

I do know you, little warrior.

Don't call me by that name.

What is your name then?

Pain flowed through his neck and legs as he stood facing this demon and gathered his breath. Demissie smiled.

A reality seeped into his features and his white teeth appeared fanged in the firelight.

Then show me who you are.

He charged and leapt over the flames and landed before Demissie, stabbing the blade through the air while Demissie eluded his attempts in easy movements. Each strike, he grunted. Energy drained from him little by little until he gave one mighty yell and charged only to fall on his knees before The Destroyer.

He raised his eyes to the calm figure over him and, atop the ridge, he saw the faint silhouettes of those he had been forbidden to speak of while in Akara land. A horde of curses complicit in their own demons.

Demissie crouched eye level with him and placed a gentle hand under his chin. He lifted the boy's face chin toward his own. A brutal tenderness in the scars on his hands. He stared, spent into the face of death and welcomed it.

What do you choose? Demissie asked.

From his knees, he exhaled and resented the tears that slid down the creases in his cheeks. His heart pulsed in his chest as if on the verge of faltering and he wondered if it should fail, would he reject such a proposition. But in his submission, in the face of the past, his mind flooded with images of bones from the Valley floating forgotten in the violence of the ancient river in graceful swirls and his spirit burned not against the Akara or Kangatum or Muhar but against life's imposition upon him and his own.

Demissie waited in his crouch and, on his knees, he turned his black eyes toward the scores of black eyes surrounding them and lifted the dirty blade. He stared intent into Demissie's face and slowly placed the tip of the blade against the boy's skin and sliced it across his chest. A black trail dripped in its wake. He bit on his lip until the cut ended and he trembled as he felt the warmth trickle down his hungry torso.

Demissie smiled and stood. He placed his massive hand and lifted the boy by his skull, ushering him to his feet. His primitive palm burned against his skin.

Then Demissie named him in the darkness, in the presence of the damned. He said the name first in a whisper, then shouted it in a deep bellow that reverberated off the rock walls and into his bones. A proclamation to creation that another had welcomed his primal calling and the words tattooed themselves, symbol by symbol, into his body until he believed his true name had been concealed from him.

He chanted his new name under his breath as his mentor in the ways of war gave a prideful smile.

Däm Afasash.

Däm Afasash.

Däm Afasash.

Like a hellish chorus, the hordes on the horizon chanted with him.

XXXV

They escorted their new recruit through the night and they continued to walk until sunrise. No mind to the beasts who emerged in the darkness.

Hunger still nagged at Däm Afasash and the opening across his chest stung and attracted flies despite the mud used to clot the bleeding.

They did not speak unless necessary. An unspoken camaraderie simmered as they marched. Only their scars spoke louder. His body and all its smooth skin made him a foreigner among them but he walked along with a desire to join those he had once abhorred for he was not the person of the village, nor the one in the cave. His salvation rested in the shadows of these nomads. He realized the blood from the night before still remained caked on his face save where the tears carved their paths. Though along the river, the deeper they embarked, the more hostile the foliage appeared. Thorns and scraggly branches reached like frail fingers across the paths made by thirsty beasts.

The band of men pushed through these sad monuments, snapping twigs against their scarred skin. No birds harbored within those empty branches and the rustle of legless bodies slithered among the yellow grass blades as their footfalls passed.

No borders or paths seemed to lead their way. An expanse of wilderness where dominion belonged to those willing to seize it.

Where are we going? Däm Afasash asked the man next to him.

The man said nothing, keeping his stolid face forward and the machete gripped in his hand.

He noticed only ten members roamed in this militia and, unable to discern if it was his memory or the fears of childhood, there had been more but he dared not ask.

Ahead, Demissie stopped and the others followed. He looked around, surveyed the harsh region and the absence of wildlife, then turned and nodded.

The others sheathed their blades and slung their rifles and began unspoken tasks. Gathering brittle sticks and hacking down logs, clearing dry grass, they moved with each aware of his purpose, his role, and moved of one accord. Däm Afasash stood as they worked. A lone stationary figure among a bustling movement.

Soon, an area had been cleared and a flint sparked a flame. Nearby large rocks had been rolled to circumvent the pit and they gathered around the fire atop their seats as the fire flicked high into the air. Each removed a small, hide casing and took bits of dried meat and sucked on them. Skins bloated with river water were passed around, even to Däm Afasash, who partook and felt the eyes watching his throat bounce down the liquid he had no business drinking. He wiped his mouth and passed it along and saw Demissie across the fire, sharpening his knife.

We rest here. We continue in land. There we will find the cockroaches.

The others chuckled when Demissie's eyes sparkled at his words and several muttered affirmations. He turned his gaze to Däm Afasash and the others turned as well. The scrappy, scarred man next to him used the tip of his blade to dig out a swollen tick in his thigh.

This is our life, little warrior. The lodgings are not as elegant as you are used to.

The peering eyes all flocked to him and the pressure they gave made his weak hands tremble. He rubbed his knees and saw the young and old figures all expectant of him as if inclined to answer. Their leader faced him, with elbows on his knees, and waited. A breeze made the fire dance and specks of dead leaves scattered across the dirt.

Däm Afasash answered, This is where I belong.

Demissie looked to the others then nodded his head to the man at Däm Afasash's left. The man handed him a strip of dried meat. His dry lips enveloped the ration and he chewed as their mendicant bodies rested.

Some slept under the new sun with arms slung over their eyes. One of the older, toothless warriors spoke with Demissie. A young boy, not much younger than he, sharpened a long, crude blade on the rock he sat on. The scrape a sharp cry that reminded him of when the old man speared a wild pig in the valley and the horrendous squeal it let loose, echoing and echoing through the hills.

Beside him, a man with his right eyelids sewn shut, looked beyond him into the sky and then pointed. Däm Afasash turned round on his seat and saw the vultures and crows circle far in the distance where the Muhar village may reside and found no other cause for the black harbingers. The image of the old man's final face gnawed at him and he turned back to the others whose faces he did not recognize from the massacre.

When facing forward, the one-eyed man had sat on the grass and dust before him. The stitches and their loose ends a grotesque image, surrounded by long, erratic scars. His one eye looked at Däm Afasash and he removed the sword from the oryx skin sheath and placed it at his side. He wore a billed cap, stained with old, dark blood. His yellow smile wide.

So you are Kelile's son? Eh? he asked. The words jovial.

Däm Afasash nodded.

I thought so. He was a great fighter. I remember, as a boy, how he killed that lion he hung over his door. Do you remember that?

I was not born yet.

Yes. Yes. I knew I wanted to do that. To be the one who could face such a killer and survive. Not only survive but conquer. You know?

Däm Afasash nodded. His chest stung and throbbed all at once.

So...what were you doing out here?

Looking for food.

Bah! You had cattle back in the Akara village and, with Kelile as your father, you wanted for nothing. Why come so far for some dried meat and good company, huh? His smile never ceased and he fiddled with the bill of his cap before swiping at flies.

Däm Afasash did not answer and looked at his swollen, dirty feet and the mud under his nails. The one-eyed man leaned forward, searching for the new recruit's face. His smile loosened as he strained forward.

I bet you are a bit shy, huh? I was shy once. Let me introduce you to these fellows.

He frog-hopped next to Däm Afasash and, next to his cheek, lifted his chin so his eyes narrowed down the barrel of his arm toward the young boy sharpening his blade.

That is Bazin. He was Hassan's boy. He was only just born when some Kangatum dogs gutted Hassan and tossed the remains in the river. Some women found him while washing.

Bazin's face glanced up as if sensing they spoke of him and his dead eyes stared blank as the long blade recited a long, agonizing scrape. Däm Afasash stared back and tried to mimic those solemn eyes but he knew behind them lurked experience beyond what he could claim. The one-eyed man chuckled and patted Däm Afasash's back enough to sting.

Good luck trying to beat him in a staring contest. No one ever has. Now, look over there, he said, shifting his outstretched arm toward another whittling at the end of long, wooden branch.

That one is Teferi. He is very mad right now because he is Muhar. You can tell by how his breath blows and his nostrils flare. Funny, huh? We came across the Muhar village massacred and burning not far back where we found you. We also found a Kangatum scout with his head bashed into pulp and then we found you. I would not want to be Kangatum when we catch up to them. Hey, Teffie!

What? he said, his voice deep like thunder.

The scarred and wrinkled face turned toward the one-eyed man. His defaced, chiseled features seemed to creak when he moved and his rippled arms rolled with his movements yet he hunched forward as if holding some heavy load upon his back. His wide eyes stared hard at the one-eyed man and Däm Afasash could not tell if they held malice or curiosity.

What did you do to that cockroach that killed your cousin? Come on, tell him. The one-eyed man leaned over and whispered, I love this story.

A perturbed expression crept into his features but, as he shaved off another sliver of wood, a hint of pride whispered through his words.

He kept his eyes. That is all.

The short man supine on his earthly bed, arm slung over his eyes, laughed through his lips. Circular scars spiraled across his torso in separate patterns and he wore dusty, green cargo pants cleanly sliced at the knees.

I told you. He's crazy that one.

Not as crazy as you, the man on the ground said without moving.

The ugly one laying in the dirt is Motuma. He is short and lazy and that is why he never had a wife.

Shut up, Mamo. You are always talking. Even in your sleep you talk.

Someone has to. What are we, animals?

Motuma waved a hand and then settled back in. Flies buzzed around his feet and Däm Afasash noticed a fresh wound sliced down his calf. The one-eyed man, now known as Mamo, leaned over close to Däm Afasash enough that his breath tickled his ear.

The short ones are always grumpy. I think it is because they are always looking up to others and they are always looking down on them. They can't win, huh?

And your name is Mamo? Däm Afasash asked.

Mamo leaned back with an expression of surprise and skepticism on his face. Are you a witch?

For the first time in days, Däm Afasash laughed. The sound nearly choked him and he covered his mouth until it passed.

Mamo smiled and slapped his hand again on Däm Afasash's back with a loud smack then shook a playful finger at his new comrade.

Ohhhh, you are full of surprises, huh? I like you, Däm Afasash.

Mamo stood up and walked over to the remaining members of the troupe seated in a circle on some sporadic rocks in the high grass. As he introduced each, he placed a congenial hand on their shoulders without consideration of their desire to be named. He started next to a stout bald man who wore a necklace of bones.

We have the great Frew who once slapped a *qäCH'ne* on the backside and got kicked in the balls. He lived to tell his story but can't have any sons.

He moved to his right and placed a presenting hand toward a lanky man so dark, his eyes appeared misplaced in his body.

This is Lemma. His is a funny story. He once killed a Kangatum dog who hid in a wanza tree without having to climb it. He just plucked him like a fruit and then broke his neck. Stand up, Lemma, so we can get a good look at you, huh?

Others laughed at the memory and Lemma rolled his eyes and stood until his full height towered over Däm Afasash and Mamo. Next to a young, toothless man whose right hand only showed two fingers, Mamo moved. The man smiled his empty grin as Mamo wrapped an arm around his shoulders.

Ahh, Adebe is a fierce one. But we call him Flower. His mother wanted a daughter and gave him his name. That is why he kills cockroaches now. Right, Flower?

Abebe nodded and patted Mamo's chest. Without moving from Abebe, he pointed at the other two who stood with their rifles slung on their back, facing the vast expanse of harsh brush inland. They did not turn and look back when Mamo's voice announced them.

Those two make the Kangatum soil their own clothes. Two makes twice the blood-shed. Hey, Etefu! Dagim! Turn around and let us look at you, eh?

The two stoic figures remained stationed and kept their gaze forward. The skin of their backs rose and sweltered with new skin. Mamo waited and then waved his hand in their direction.

Ahh, they are so serious those two. Never smile or enjoy life. You tell them a joke and they look at you like two stupid dogs. They only smile when they find their enemy. Unlike us, huh?

He rotated and addressed the group who all appeased the gregarious spokesman with patronizing grunts.

Mamo! Demissie called.

He straightened and faced toward the god-like stature of their leader. The jovial countenance at once gone and his place among the militia established by the mere timbre of his voice.

Arm him, he instructed.

Mamo nodded and marched toward the cache of weapons laid in the center of the group. Weapons of the valley, of every tribe and people, lay beckoning. Muhar, Akara, Kangatum, the whites. Even an Omaro bow, as ancient as the extinct tribe it belonged to. Most stained from their experience.

Demissie's eyes affixed to Däm Afasash and his baleful stare caused his body to shift for reasons he knew not why. He kept his eyes on Mamo but could not ignore the penetration of Demissie's yellow-black eyes.

Mamo grabbed Däm Afasash's shoulders and squared up to him. His eyes examined the features of the new recruit. Mamo's tongue poked from the side of his mouth, giving him a comical, rabid look he had seen on mad dogs.

After a moment, Mamo seemed to speak to himself.

Let's see. A man's weapon is very important. It is part of him. Unique to him, yes? So what type of weapon belongs to you? What do your eyes tell me?

Däm Afasash only stared back, perplexed but patient. A light flickered on Mamo's face and he bent over the cache and sifted through the weaponry. Soon, he grabbed two sheathed machetes and stood, facing Däm Afasash again with a pleased smile.

These are your weapons. I can see it in your eyes.

He thrust the blades into his hands. Däm Afasash looked uneasy into Mamo's face. The laughter of such a morbid task, of joy and murder so intricately entwined puzzled him and he knew not what was real or a nightmare.

He took the blades and held them in his hands as the reality of his situation descended upon him. The weight of those blades still felt after he slipped his arms through the sheaths and hung them, crossways, across his back.

The others finished their food and gathered their weapons. Grim countenances all around as Demissie trundled through the group. The inspection signaled by the way he carried his head until he reached the twins at the outskirts. He stopped and looked over Etefu and Dagim beyond the horizon. Wind bent the grass at their feet. The miscellany of arms he bore morphed him into something beyond comprehension. A mutant spirit of war deformed by its own being.

Demissie turned back to his following. Eyes engorged with a thirst unquenchable that lit the daylight and reigned upon the land, demanding submission from all creation. In Däm Afasash's eyes, he bore many names with many duties. Wanted and unwanted. Destroyer. Judge. Executioner. God.

He bellowed his command and, perhaps, the earth truly did tremble at his malevolence.

We walk.

XXXVI

They marched on, carried like ghosts in the wind, feet slicing through yellow, knee-high grass and delving further across the plains toward the shadows of the forest.

The ragged group fanned out in formation. Motuma kept his eyes skyward as vultures circled overhead and ravens cried their raucous calls. Däm Afasash placed among the group. Faces from what seemed so long ago, somewhere between dreams and reality, and he often glanced behind him at the receding river and convinced himself that his father and mother marched behind them, arm in arm with the old man, calling his old name. But he would not answer.

Mamo kept his one good eye out for Däm Afasash from the fringe of the flank. His boisterous voice silenced as they followed the messy tracks of the Kangatum raiders. Dagim and Etefu led the way with eyes sharp to the ground with Demissie not far behind.

The machetes on Däm Afasash's back protruded like horns in his shadow and, with his weapons attached to him, the wandering in his heart faded.

They stopped only to drink from the skin canteens and consume small, strips of meat or berries found along the way. His soles ached and the silence remained. Though Mamo came by, he only winked.

Rested, they marched further into the dry brush. The sharp sticks and twigs scraped against their scarred bodies as they maneuvered their own trails. The twins and Demissie often paused and huddled in whispers before changing course, pointing at unseen marks in the dust.

In the claustrophobic foliage, Däm Afasash kept his eyes affixed on the others. On Lemma or Teferi. Even the child-like face of Bazin and his dead eyes. Anything to keep from succumbing to separation in the vastness of the land.

They snaked their way in this labyrinth, crouched and taut, until the twins froze and bony fingers guided their attention to a small, clearing.

Demissie stepped forward. Even crouched, he towered over those two, and his grave head nodded. The others had funneled close together and collapsed on Däm Afasash's space until he could feel their breath and smell the musk of their sour bodies in the cramped space. The faint sound of chatter rose in the distance.

We will wait for tonight. Lemma, Mamo, Bazin, and Teferi will go to the other side of the clearing. Motuma, Abebe, and Frew, to the left. Dagim and Etefu will wait at the right. Little warrior, you wait with me here.

When his words ended, the designated groups dispersed and slipped soundless into the thickets and brush until only the faint hum of their fleeting presence remained.

Demissie crouched on his haunches like a massive beast nestled in the bush and Däm Afasash crept close beside him. Demissie pointed and he could see, from a small window, a horde of familiar Kangatum faces and the bounty of their plunder piled among them. Several still wore caked blood from their raid on their milky white skin. Shirts darkened and pants soaked. Several lay in repose on woven mats taken from their victims. A cache of Muhar and Akara weapons jutted from the plunder. Every Kangatum soldier's waistband held a pistol or nestled a rifle in the crook of their arm, whether standing or asleep. Smoke spiraled from their cooking fires.

Däm Afasash knew the smell and the memory of the old man and the massacre they witnessed renewed fresh in his vision. A rancor at the sight of such merciless creatures stirred inside him and the weight of his blades seared into his back.

Bouts of laughter broke out among the group and the taut air sizzled in the brush. A group of dejected children, wrists and ankles tied, sat on the fringes with downcast heads and he saw the same faces from the massacre which seemed so long ago.

A hand startled him and he turned to see Demissie's still eyes. He engulfed the small space and he leaned in close toward Däm Afasash.

Vengeance is patient. Anger will betray you.

Their eyes remained locked a moment before several Kangatum warriors gave a loud, jubilant hoot and fired several rounds into the air in stuttering bursts. The captives cowered and shrieked, prompting chuckles from their captors. They waited in the fading afternoon light and watched. Däm Afasash's foot began to tingle and he readjusted as the needles pricked under his skin.

He watched as the Kangatum spoke to one another and bragged of how many lives they had taken or how many women they took for themselves, of the way they would scar their body to illustrate their worth, how the old men cried before they shot them and the humorous way in which they fell. They mimicked the cries of the young children and those mothers who begged for mercy. A crowd of jokers who found what creation deemed evil a cause for laughter.

As the flames grew and the daylight draped them toward darkness, Däm Afasash watched with growing malice as the final face of the old man looped in his head. The cycle continued in his thoughts until he muttered without being aware.

They are evil.

Demissie grunted. There is no evil, little warrior. There is no good either. The gods have abandoned us to our own will and the will of man has only one mission and that is for vindication.

But I have seen what they have done. I was there when they slaughtered the Muhar village.

Only blood can wash away blood.

They started this. Those cockroaches attacked women and children and old men.

Demissie spit at his feet. How can we claim when blood was spilled first?

Däm Afasash turned to him. You defend them?

I do not. But I do not make myself out to be the hand of justice. I was created to fight and I will make my creator proud. It is the life I have chosen. Your father was the same way but he would not do what needed to be done in order to protect his own.

You don't know.

Our threat lies beyond these bushes and it is my duty to destroy it. As a leader, your father should be here. To protect the Akara and our allies. But he chose you and Wagaye.

Demissie's words against his father added to his building rage. My father is a good man and a great Akara.

He is too good. When I found you by the river, I could see in your eye you had changed. The look was in you. You have tasted and now you have the thirst.

Däm Afasash shook his head.

I feel no thirst.

Demissie, for the first time, turned from the Kangatum, and a slow smile crept on his face. The deep voice boomed in a whisper.

Yet here you wait.

The air fumed around them huddled in the bush as if their very breaths and the words they carried released fire. The dawn of a baleful epiphany rose in his mind and he forced a swallow in his dry throat.

Demissie's black eyes seemed to dilate and the satisfaction imbued in his gothic features revealed the truth. Däm Afasash turned away and dwelled on those words as he watched the Kangatum through his crude window, unable to see the others circling their prey.

Demissie leaned close to the boy and spoke as if in a whisper a saying he recalled from his youth.

It is better to die than to live without killing.

The guerrillas remained cramped as darkness settled in. The Kangatum warriors feasted on their plunder and drank beer from metal canteens they acquired from the whites who sold them guns. A reddish fire blazed in the clearing and a wiry man so etched with scars threw huge bundles of dried brush on the fire until the flames licked the sky above the foliage. Slouched in celebration and drink, the band of raiders reveled in their own power and chanted ancient songs from their tribe and beyond. Some songs Däm Afasash recalled around the Akara fires and he could still see the dancers, plumed in feathers and leaves, shake their bodies and thrust their arms skyward as they danced around the fire before invisible gods. But the scene before him bore no ceremony.

Däm Afasash felt the night tug at him and an anxiousness settled in his hands and feet.

He glanced at Demissie with the hope that his face would indicate it was time but no such look was given. Instead, Demissie's brutal face stared intent into the heart of the clearing and the glow appeared to pour down his face.

The drink had caused the celebration to diminish as, one by one, the Kangatum dropped off into sleep. Either propped against a rock or supine in the dirt with canteens still gripped. Even the wiry man had stopped his continual feeding of the fire and dozed in halting nods.

They continued to wait until only a murmur whispered among the drunken and the howls and shrieks of creation echoed atop the brush.

Again, Däm Afasash looked to Demissie. The tension mounted so high within him he feared he may weep. Yet they waited.

After a time, he leaned forward and whispered, When?

Demissie did not reply.

The sizzle of burning sticks frazzled the air. Though no human words spoke, the noise around them seemed deafening.

As if the earth carried a sixth sense of when blood would be spilled. A prophecy soon to be fulfilled that nature awaited and grew restless at the waiting.

Then all fell silent.

Demissie gave a whistle and, in a crash of fury, they burst from the bush like a horde of demons. Weapons held high in the darkness that shattered the silence. The cry shook Däm Afasash's very moorings and fear rose in him at the thought of being the recipient of such violence.

Drunken and confused, the raiders stumbled and fell with eyes wide and uncomprehending as the warriors descended upon them.

A Kangatum who had gone to relive himself by the brush contorted back as Motuma's club pummeled through bone and teeth high in a spray of some twisted confetti.

Frightened raiders scrambled for their guns only to have the twins descend upon their crawling backs. Their cries muffled in the dust as their feet held their heads down and pierced those scarred backs over and over.

Däm Afasash was the last to leave the bush and moved as if in a dream and watched the carnage outside himself. The helpless Kangatum raised their feeble hands only to have those very hands separate and fall to the dust.

Teferi's massive arms pressed into a man's neck as the eyes bulged from the sockets and Däm Afasash recoiled at the unnatural color. The calm intensity in Teferi's face while the man clutched and thrashed at those unmoving arms appeared normal among the bloodshed.

A Kangatum managed to fetch a spear and stabbed Teferi in the shoulder but he only flinched and crushed the man in his arms before turning toward his assailant. The man turned and fled into the arms of Frew and let loose such a shriek, Frew began to laugh.

The chaos churned with each death. The presence of those machetes on his back and the vision of death by the river engulfed him.

He watched motionless.

The bound children screamed as the men of his own tribe moved in graceful sweeps and resembled an artist at work upon the canvas. An arrow flew clean through a Kangatum eye from Bazin's bow. The cold stare never leaving his face.

Mamo snuck upon a Kangatum ready to deliver a strike upon Abebe's head and sliced the ready arm, landing still cocked in the dust. A gunshot rang out and Lemma staggered backward, clutching his gut. The crack of the bullet resounded in Däm Afasash's ear and he saw the Kangatum boy, eyes glossed and vacant, struggle at the locked bolt in frantic indecision. As the bullet still echoed, Däm Afasash felt the spirit of his nature overtake him and in two giant steps he crashed into the boy and those thirsty machetes rose above his head and came down. The familiar warmth showered Däm Afasash's face at the hacked body at his feet. His breath heaved as the blood streamed into his eyes but did not burn. He looked back to the killing and saw Demissie still. A proud stare lit on his face in the fire glow.

The cries had waned until only the pleading voice of a lone Kangatum warrior, aged and grey and soaked with the vitals of his kinsmen, cowered on his back. His arms raised in futile defense as Demissie and Teferi loomed over him with dark droplets falling from their chins and hands. The Kangatum man began to weep and, in his own tongue, begged for mercy.

Let me do it, Teferi asked.

Demissie knelt down in front the man. He froze and his lips trembled. Demissie smeared the blood on his face and snapped his hand toward the dirt.

You go back. Tell them what has happened and that death is coming.

A relief surfaced on the man's face for a brief moment until Demissie removed a long, stained blade from his belt and took the man's hand in one sweep. A final shout rattled the brush and the man writhed in the dirt among the fallen.

Go, my messenger. Tell my story, Demissie shouted and kicked at the man as if to shoo a dog until he stumbled to his feet and disappeared through the brush, staining the earth as he left.

A groan came from behind and Lemma lay propped against some Kangatum bodies clutching his belly with red hands.

Demissie and the others approached as he took shallow breaths. His eyes closed while the flies moved in. A grave silence surrounded the group before Mamo whispered something into Demissie's ear.

With the blade still in his hand, Demissie crouched close to Lemma and spoke a prayer into his ear. Lemma nodded, appearing half-asleep. He did not make a sound as Demissie slid the blade under his chin. Däm Afasash watched as Lemma shook then ceased to move. The ceremony solemn in a moment of silence before they turned their bloodshot eyes and began to gather their plunder.

The others sifted through the dead bodies for weapons or food while others searched the skins and baggage. Abebe and Mamo stacked mounds of dried brush and sticks on the fires not doused by blood until the flames rose high and hot. Then they lifted Lemma and tossed the body onto the pyre. The smell of burnt hair and flesh and smoky wood filled the night.

Mamo's voice lifted and he sang an old Akara funeral song asking for a safe journey to the afterlife that Däm Afasash remembered as a child. All gathered around the growing fire and joined in voice as the flames licked at the night sky. Their chorus not rife with mourning but of celebration for a fallen warrior who died an idyllic death. The song carried upward and Däm Afasash stared deep into the fire and watched the yellow and orange swirl together to form flashes of red.

Beyond the song, a thud worked its way between the melody and he looked up and, caught by the fringe of the firelight, he saw Demissie patrolling the Kangatum bodies. He approached each and swung his blade down on the necks of the fallen and then moved on to the next. Outside of the firelight, Däm Afasash watched the faint outline of his fellow Akara warrior, indistinct in the darkness, diligent at the work assigned to himself.

Mamo's lone song rose higher and louder and then he saw the work of Demissie's hand. Like a body birthed from the darkness, the blood soaked figure walked forward, bathed in firelight. Each hand carried heads with frozen faces. His fingers wrapped around the soulless jaws with the demeanor of a man carrying buckets of water to his dwelling.

The funeral song carried across flame and wind and sky and, for the briefest of moments, Däm Afasash believed the song came from the very mouths Demissie carried.

The song ended and the birth of dawn arrived just above the mountains. Demissie, soaked, walked toward the group, placed the faces toward the fire then pointed in the direction toward the river.

We move now.

Without protest, the group gathered their plunder and artillery. Demissie stood by Däm Afasash and cast his empty gaze.

What about them? he asked, pointing to the trembling children bound together.

They have each other.

But they may die out here.

Demissie nodded and placed a paternal hand on his shoulder.

As will we.

Then headed past him.

The group marched single file through the water trail paved by oryx. One by one, the warriors disappeared into the brush as silent as they arrived until only Däm Afasash remained among the carnage. Vultures circled overhead and a host of hungry creatures waited as he looked back upon the work of his hands. His lone victim's face retained the very look when his life left him and Däm Afasash wondered if that Kangatum's final thought still remained in his head.

He turned and looked into the terrified faces huddled outside the pyre. Torn between his new calling and the innocence of youth. The children said nothing but their faces screamed for him.

Looking at where the horde had disappeared, he ran over and dropped one of his machetes by the boy he remembered from before. The young, wet eyes stared at the blade and then Däm Afasash.

Then he turned and sprinted into the bush.

XXXVII

The trail carved through the bush and the ashes of Lemma floated above the thickets into the morning skyline. The smell of smoke followed them as they marched.

He hung to the rear and watched Mamo's back as it disappeared then reappeared around the bends. Mamo had given him some bread from the plunder but, despite the ache in his belly, he could not eat it for it turned to ash in his mouth.

Droppings littered the trail and Däm Afasash wondered if this road would ever end. Now consumed in the act he hated, he had never felt so detached from his own body. As if his bones were not his own.

He spat into his palms and scrubbed at the dried blood but it only smeared and meshed on his dark skin and he thought, in the faintest recesses of his mind, he heard the old man call him. Not in anger, but like the man before the fire in the shadow of the river.

His head pounded and his walk staggered as the sharp branches scratched deep into his skin. As he followed the group, he was back in the brush. The quick, lithe figure of Dawit scampered ahead and he struggled to keep up as they emerged, eyes cast upon the Valley. Eyes transfixed on the barrenness and the scavengers feasting on what could have been friends and he may or may not have vowed to not be Akara but his memory failed him.

They had made their way back toward the river and the grasslands fanned toward the sheer rock faces of the Omo in the distance. The others marched before him, all visible in the fresh sunlight, painted and trailed by the buzz of flies. Once out of the brush, the jovial voice of Mamo returned.

What a mess we are, huh? I can't wait to get in that river and wash this Kangatum filth off me. Right, Bazin?

Bazin's cold stare did not acknowledge him.

Däm Afasash saw a snake slither off, waving the grass blades in escape. Mamo turned back and looked at him.

So you got one, huh?

Däm Afasash glanced back at Mamo's one, vibrant eye and nodded.

Good, good. Cut them down like the cockroaches they are.

Unable to determine if it were a lack of food or exhaustion, Däm Afasash stumbled a bit, placing a hand on his temple. Mamo slowed and slipped the goat skin off his shoulder and loosened the cinch.

Drink this. You trying to die or something?

He poured warm water down Däm Afasash's throat and he could feel the wetness flow through his chest and such relief filled him. The water flowed too fast and he coughed. Laughs from the others intermittent between heaps for air.

You need to eat and drink. This land isn't as nice as we are.

Däm Afasash coughed once more and then handed the goatskin to Mamo who pushed it back to him.

You keep it.

I couldn't save Lemma, he said in a hoarse tone.

We don't speak of the lost.

Why not?

Mamo looked ahead at the others well ahead. Love can kill out here. We must forget or it is us who will be smoke.

He nodded toward the black curls still rising from far in the brush.

Then how will you remember them?

Däm Afasash thought he saw a shadow pass over Mamo's one good eye.

We don't.

They walked in tandem like a ragged, blood-stained caravan stalking the land. The twins led with Demissie and walked with restless eyes. Heads swiveled across the vast plain for any sign. Teferi and Frew slapped at their ears when the flies tickled them.

The river inched closer.

How did you end up here? With them? Däm Afasash asked.

Mamo did not answer for several steps before he spoke.

Have you ever watched the lions?

Däm Afasash shook his head.

When a male lion takes over a pride, he kills all the cubs. Do you know why he does this, huh?

No.

He wants to clean out the other leader's bloodline. You see? He doesn't ask the lioness and the lioness does not interfere because this is the way things are. It is what they are supposed to do. No one questions why hippos swim or why flies eat dung. Would you ask a man why he breathes? Huh? Because you know it is what we all must do. It is how the gods made it to be. My children know this. So did my wife.

The aged warrior paused before muttering, In the end, we all will be smoke.

Mamo smiled after he finished and slapped a congenial hand on the back of the new recruit. The words stuck to him and something primordial pierced him in their tone as if the syllables aimed to both encourage and destroy him at once.

The roar of water rose as the tall, sheer rockface jutted from the violent churning below. When they reached the embankment, they slid down with dust caking the sweat and blood on their dark bodies. They approached the water's edge and began to wash themselves.

As Däm Afasash watched, he noticed the wounded neither dressed nor acknowledged their wounds. Frew's open flesh revealed muscle as he dipped into the murky water. Bazin, standing to his ankles, refused to clean the Kangatum blood from his body and only cupped water in his hands to slake his thirst. Mamo trotted into the water, feet kicking up sprays and noise.

Stop with your shit, Mamo. We don't need *gumare* here.

Mamo leaned over and flicked water into Abebe's face and chuckled to himself.

Relax, huh?

Abebe glared and resumed his washing.

Waded to his waist, Demissie's torso emerged from the water, nearly forged from the very rocks he stood before and bathed out in the brackish Omo like a warrior defiant of all creation's laws. Disregard for predators and any hierarchy nature sought to impose.

Däm Afasash left his weapon on the shore and waded to his knees. He flung water onto his body and scrubbed at his skin in a frantic washing. Despite his efforts, he still felt blood on his face, on his hands, on his chest. He examined his dripping hands and saw only blood on the pale palms.

Through wet eyes, he watched Demissie and, at once, admired and feared the man before him. The same blood within and out stained both their bodies and, knee deep in the river, he sucked air as if he were drowning.

Atop the water's surface, the blank stare of the Kangatum boy floated by, mouth agape in death, followed by Dawit and Dunga and the countless others. From the water, the depths of his past bubbled to the surface and terrible eyes watched him.

His mother's eyes melted tears into the waves.

The old man's grim pupils swollen before his final blade, and their agape mouths all called his names.

Tesfahun, Gägäma. Tessie. Däm Afasash.

Different names all his own.

Names bound to the past he could not outrun. His new name impossible to wash off. A flash of shame overwhelmed him and his eyes welled with tears as the others stood bathing.

Mamo stood and arched his back as a stream flowed from him into the river. Motuma sat in the shallows and rested back on his straightened arms, face upward. Around him was death and all its friends.

Then the unholy tatter of guns rang through the morning mist. He saw Mamo's face sicken as blood flowed from holes drilled through his back and he fell to the water in a posture unknown to the living. Bodies and sprays of water moved around him in a dance. New comrades fell into the water and others scrambled for their weapons abandoned on the shore only to jerk and contort face first below the waves.

A Kangatum war cry burst in the gorge. He searched but could not see Demissie or those who shot them. The skull of one of the twins burst open with a pop and its contents plopped in the river like a spoiled fruit.

He stood paralyzed in the river. Moans and cries carried across the waters and up the steep ravines, chased by the blast of rounds. His only thought that perhaps, he truly was mingi and his curse had found him.

Then a fiery pain tore through his shoulder. Warmth poured down his chest. Fresh blood, his own blood, ran down his body into the water and he wondered in this perilous moment if the gods had come to exact revenge for the blood he had taken.

As if jolted, his body awakened and legs sprinted into the river, deeper and deeper until his wound submerged and water poured into his nostrils.

Muted gunfire continued above the surface. Floating in the water, he saw Bazin's lifeless eyes as stern in death as in life. The figure drifted with the current as if ferried by the souls before him.

The water quickened and its force took him and Bazin down the current and dragged them under trailing blood in their wake.

He bobbed above the surface enough to catch a breath before being sucked under. On one last surface, he cried out for help and felt the power of a boulder against the back of his skull. The light snuffed from his eyes and he floated without resistance where ever the river would take him.

PART IV

Life has no meaning for one without a home.

XXXVIII

Dawit is there. They splash in the shallows of the cool, murky water below their navel and the sun settles overhead. Dawit places his slick hands across his neck and the boys grapple and laugh. Heads push under only to resurface and he stares at the shore under the shade of the wanza and waves to father and mother sitting on a fallen log. Bale stands behind them and waves and he can see her smile from the water. Even Ogbay, sturdy and clear eyed, leans against the bark and waves. Waves from the water and The Old Man sits in the grass with his elbows perched on his knees and the fresh blood tainting the white hairs of his chin and he calls to them from the river but they only wave. He turns back to Dawit and Dunga is there now soaked in blood and Dawit holds him around the waist and looks up but Dunga only stares at him. He calls out but his stoic countenance and dead eyes fixed his way. He looks back to the wanza but they only wave and he does not know for what purpose. Something trembles the water and he whips around and before him a figure surfaces from the ripples and rises like some demon from the depths and Demissie's body pours forth the river and blood combined as his scarred body rises and rises until his shadow casts across the length of the river. Then the children rise. One at first and then the others. Self-exhumed from the forgotten bowels of the river bottom and the faces he never knew sprout for the first time across the waters and he is surrounded on all sides by discarded youth. The others continue to wave from the shade of the wanza and then the chorus of their voices echoes toward him across the water and they call his names like a baleful symphony and his voice cries out to join them but is as muted as the river swallows his voice. Now the names, his names, crash and collide until he cannot decipher who speaks which name and a cry splits from his mouth and he splashes, spinning panic in his eyes and spins and spins and turns until he stops, somehow, and stands in the water with an image like his own face to face. The curve of the nose, the high cheekbones, bloodshot eyes. He sees him for the first time and then tears flow and he reaches out to take him into his arms but there is nothing but water and he falls forward, through the body, and plunges into the waters in a blast of painful white and he suspends in this cavern unable to see nor feel and in the distance voices carry through the water, indecipherable and foreign, calling and crying and gnashing and he raises his slow hands to his ears but they continue to call, to sing, to cry on and on and on...

XXXIX

Sunlight assaulted his retinas.

Dark feminine faces leaned over his body with busy hands. White cloths draped over their shoulders. His head rolled with water and the pain replaced the brilliance behind his eyes and the memory of the river returned. Dried leaves rustled under his slightest move. A deep throb afire buried into his shoulder and he recoiled as a gentle hand pushed him back to the cot.

"Don't move. We will be there soon."

Her soft voice flowed through the waters of his ears and he closed his eyes.

He opened looked up as clouds passed behind their pursed faces and an overhang of swooping trees broke the banality of the sky. Their heavy breaths in rhythm with their steps.

He wondered if the mingi had found him guilty and now carried him to the river to atone for his sins. Perhaps lead by his brother. A procession of ghosts bent on retribution and vindication for each other. He knew he would not struggle. Perhaps they wished to take him to the Valley instead and take his place among the nameless. Either outcome, he welcomed a place free of blood.

His head lolled side to side as the boys' grip weakened. One stumbled and the others nails dug into his wounded side and he cried out, tasting the saltiness of sweat on his tongue. The boys murmured to one another and his lids closed again as their pace quickened, rocking his fragile body to sleep.

He awoke to a soft breeze. Outside a window, he saw the lithe figures of boys and girls scatter around a dusty, packed patch of earth as their nimble feet kicked a checkered ball. Skirts flared as the girls chased boys with unknown emblems on their chests. The shrill, ecstatic laughs carried to him and he tried to lift his head to watch but his head ached beyond comprehension.

"Sleep. Do not stand."

The strange accent spoke Muhar. He rolled his head away from the window and saw a room surrounded by brown plaster and a table stacked with bandages, bottles, and books.

A man, pale as fire, skin smooth and free of blemish, stood at the table with his head turned back to him. He smiled and poured liquid from a brown bottle onto a white cloth. While the man worked, he tried to search for the one who spoke in tribal tongues. His weak eyes strained to the edges of his vision but saw no one but the white man and his mysterious elixir.

The man finished at the table and approached him and he cowered back and tried to speak only to feel the pierce of his parched lips tearing.

"Settle. No need to do move. You are safe," the man said in Kangatum.

He stared at this pale man and his red shirt and blue pants. The dirt brown of his hair and how it hung straight to his ears. The man examined the patient's face and then took the soiled cloth and placed it on the wound. The sting surged through his body and he kicked out, knocking a cup by the cot. He recalled the pale faces from the village and their black boxes from a time he could not measure.

Don't kill me! he exclaimed.

"Ok. It's Ok. Settle calm," he assured in Akara, pressing down on the wound hard.

When his eyes refocused, he looked at the white man hunched over him.

How do you speak Akara? he asked.

"I learn it."

For a moment, he forgot the pain and a dry laugh escaped his throat. The white man's stoic face stayed intent on dressing the wound as he asked, "Why you laugh?"

His laugh tripped to a cough before he answered. I never knew a white man could speak my language.

"We are filled with surprises," he tried to say but the sounds coalesced in a comical sequence. "I know I am bad but I do it. You learn my words?"

The pain returned and he grimaced. Muscles tensed along the plank of his battered body. The man's hands lifted and hovered above his wound until the tension passed then he continued with delicate hands.

Did I die? he asked after a hard swallow.

"No, no no. The girls found on the river. Rebecca tell me you hurt."

The solid roof was of the same substance as the walls and he turned his head toward the window. Beyond the children, low-lying mountains paralleled the river and the sound of bullets and water splashing came to him and he wondered had anyone but him escaped from the ambush.

From his bed, the mountains sat in the distance but the faces of those scattered children blocked them from view. A warmth filled him as he watched. Some girls held a rope and jumped as others swung. The girl in the middle alternated feet as she hopped. Boys chased one another with teeth bared. Every face dimpled and full of pure, white teeth.

He looked back but the white man had left. He raised his head up and searched only to find a thick book propped on the table, surrounded by medical supplies. He stared at the book and remembered how the whites who came, led by countrymen clothed as whites, carried books full of pictures and maps along with their flashing cameras to the village.

Noise came from the door and the white man returned. Under his arms, the shirt darkened and clung to his side as he wiped his forehead with the back of his hand. He returned to the table, wrapping a long, mesh cloth around his hand.

"Looks like you will cure – Sorry what is your name?" he asked.

Such a simple question would have been easier for anyone but he to answer but he could not find one that belonged to him. His lip trembled silent. The white man paused and glanced back with a wave of his brow and saw something on his patient's face that burdened him.

"No worry," he said, finishing up his business with the cloth, "we will find you one."

He watched the white man approach a moment. A severe stare born in those blue eyes and he asked, Is that book about me?

The white man paused while a slight smile shaped his lips. "It about all of us."

A heavy crease weighted his brow looking up into this new face, more white than any he had ever seen during his time in the village. Whiter than the bones under his feet in the Valley. Yet in the bizarre pallor, there shone something he had rarely known. So rare he could not name it.

His strength slipped from him and he laid his aching head down and faded to sleep with the sounds of laughing children.

He awoke in the same hut where he met the white man with no name. Time disoriented in his mind. Despite the suns low place above the mountains, he could not tell if twilight or dawn had come. The children out his window had all gone and an empty courtyard remained save the checkered ball resting in the center of the dirt.

He lifted his head and felt fire surge throughout his chest. Mesh cloths and tape clung across his moist skin and concealed the wound as flies buzzed at the open flesh underneath.

When he flexed his stomach to sit up, the pain pushed him back with such force his head bounced off the cot. He breathed heavy through his nostrils and drifted through memory. Thrust into those moments that flashed as if he had not lived them himself. His mother's moist eyes a backdrop to these past visions.

The fire in his chest turned to nausea and he leaned to his side and vomited though he did not recall eating the tainted mush now splattered on the dirt floor.

Soft footsteps approached as he rolled back and waited for the white man. Instead, a woman entered. Curly black hair hung from under her head wrap and her cheekbones, high and soft, rested like clouds under her eyes. She wore a dress patterned of flowers that graced the top of her toes when she walked. Those eyes flashed at him and then, somber-faced, she gathered items at the table.

From behind, he watched her and saw her earlobes, whole and smooth. She turned and his eyes darted elsewhere. With a brown bottle in one hand and a roll of gauze in the other, she walked toward the cot, still lipped and head high, and began to undress the wound on his chest.

He watched the delicate movements of her hands and marveled at how it was as if she did not touch him at all. Her eyes remained on the task at hand.

Are you one of the girls who took me from the river? he asked.

She nodded.

You speak Akara?

She balled the pink stained cloth in her palm and then nodded again. Her eyes still remained on the wound.

What is this place?

A place where you can get help. Preacher is a very caring man. He cares for all of us in more ways than just our bodies.

All of you?

Yes. The children.

He turned his head at the ghostly yard.

Where have they gone?

To school. Here, Preacher teaches us how to read and write in English and about God.

Which one?

She looked at him for the first time since she spoke. A callous, puzzled expression bordering on annoyance.

What do you mean?

Which god?

There is only one God.

Such an outlandish notion paralyzed him, more so than the hole in his shoulder. She noticed his confusion but said nothing and returned to her work.

He recalled the Kings and the skulls and bones tacked to the fence around their sacred huts and a part of him had unwavering faith in the pantheon of his raised religion. But the Valley centered in his being and dismantled what he once knew as faith.

One god, he stated under his breath.

She inspected the exposed wound. A swollen red myriad of carnage. She shook her head and conveyed a sunken expression of such disappointment, he forgot of this one god and asked, Why do you shake your head?

Her nimble hands folded the gauze into a flat square in deliberate movements.

I do not understand why men would make weapons that can do such damage.

His eyes fixed on her face.

The white man brought those guns, he said.

She shook her head as she worked.

No. Man did.

That is just how it has always been.

She looked at him. Hands still. Her eyes appeared to broaden so much that he felt they may swallow him.

But that is not how it has to be. Not anymore.

He kept his eyes on her. What is your name?

The expansive eyes shrunk back and she reached over and grabbed a roll of tape and scratched at the end.

Rebecca.

What is your real name?

That is my real name.

Not a white man name. The Akara name given to you by your people.

She exhaled through her nose and the tape tore as she pulled long strands and placed them across the folded gauze. The faint flex of her jawbone broke her stony expression.

Whatever that name was, it is not my name now. I am Rebecca and always will be.

Another tear of tape and she pressed the adhesive hard on the gauze and he flinched. She finished the front before the pain had subsided.

Turn over.

He struggled to his side but his body froze before falling onto his back again. She sighed, placed the tape on the table and pushed him over onto his stomach. He rolled hard and landed on his belly, aggravating the bruise on his skull as his face smashed into the cot.

She ignored his moans and returned to the table, dipped a cloth in water, and cleaned the wound. He rested his chin on his hands and saw, out the window, a new perspective of more plaster buildings.

What are those buildings over there? he said.

There is the chapel on the other side where we have church on Sunday.

Are all these children yours? Or do they belong to the white man?

A giggle escaped her lips but as she dipped the bloody cloth in the bowl.

That would be quite a lot of children for me to have by my eighteenth year. Do I look that old to you?

He laughed and then grimaced at the pain of each spasm.

Stop that. You will hurt yourself.

Faint voices came from behind those walls as if speaking a chant or recitation but he did not know the words. The chorus of young voices sent him back to playing mamba among the huts in the warm breeze that blew across his naked body and Dawit pounced on his back and they toppled into the dust and sucked sugar cane stalks while Wagaye and Bale mashed sorghum in stone mortars.

So where do they come from?

He felt the tickle on his back as she folded the gauze across his spine.

They are the forgotten children. Some lost parents to disease. But most have been saved from their own kind. From the river and the bush.

His pain mingled with an overbearing burden among the chorus. He wondered, perhaps, if maybe this one god had captured him and sent him here for a reason. He swallowed back the saliva into his throat.

Are you? he asked.

Her hands laid the gauze down and hovered above the wound. The tips trembled as if she cast some magic over him. She licked her dry lips before the words breathed into the air and carried like an unspoken secret exposed.

I am *mingi*, she whispered.

He turned his head to look at her once more but a rush of screaming children poured from the buildings and into the yard.

"How are our visitor?"

He turned back and saw the white man enter and Rebecca slipped out the door, passing Preacher on her.

His full face leaned in and examined the wound and a clack ticked from the back of his throat.

"Well, it gone through so you should heal in good. Just rest is all you need. Did Rebecca help you?"

He nodded and Preacher straightened his back and placed his palms on his hips, arching as if his hands supported such a movement. He looked up at his caretaker, so different from the old man and the cave and more distant from Demissie and all he represented and even beyond him to the Akara. A fleeting vision of his father striking a spear through that exposed, luminescent belly came and went and he felt nothing stir within him. He looked past Preacher but did not see her return.

"I will end the wound and then have someone bring food," he said with a smile.

Looking around, he saw the tape and began dressing the wound. He whistled while he placed strips on his back as he laid facedown. The intrinsic notion of being watched came over him and he turned his head back to the window to two bright eyed faces peeking over the sill.

They stared at one another but their white eyes held no fear. Only curiosity. Two boys far from their initiations. Minds walled within, impenetrable to the hands that would snatch them without consequence and cast their growing bodies into the depths or let them slip into spirit in valleys and expanses where no horizon dare show itself. Nor would those eyes comprehend the power of their own hands. To feel the weight of weaponry slated across their backs and the burden of vengeance that flows within the confines of their veins. Their eyes squinted and darted here and there until Preacher returned.

"Get out of here, rascals," he said, shooing them with his hands.

The boys stood and fled, arms flailing and laughter in their wake. He watched them return to the others and felt something stir within him he had forgotten long ago.

"There," Preacher said and stepped back, "You can lay backward now."

He couldn't help but chuckle as Preacher helped turn him over and ease him onto his back again.

"What is funny?"

He coughed several times. Your Akara is terrible.

Preacher's harried eyes looked down at him a moment, hands on his hips again. Then a smile crept across his face and his chest bounced with a silent laughter.

"Yes, is bad. Maybe you will learn me and I can learn you my words," he said.

Preacher reached out and lifted his hand and held it in his palms as if cradling a sacred object. From the cot, he stared at the dark and light hands mingled together.

Preacher returned his hand to the cot. "Do you know a name?"

What do you mean?

Preacher paused and searched for the right word.

"You name?"

He turned his face from the white man and looked out the window. Preacher clicked his throat again while behind his eyes he pondered some mystery.

"I know your name," he said.

He looked back to the man who waited with a severity in those blue eyes. A color that washed over like a baptism. The color of his savior in the land of forgotten children. His breath stayed in his lungs.

"Your name is Moses."

No such name had graced his ears. The timbre of it whispered into his bones in a manner breathed from a divinity far from the spirits of his youth or the cave or of the land. He knew not what it meant, but he exhaled, feeling the pressure leave his wounded chest and with it, he whispered his new name. Despite this stirring, in his mind, Moses was another name upon his list.

Why Moses? He asked.

"Because you come from river."

XL

He spied her as she walked by his window across the yard but those hypnotic eyes never turned his way.

Children bearing a mixture of scrapes and bruises trickled in and had their wounds nursed by an older woman whose hands mirrored that of a man. Her leathery skin pulled tight as if her bones struggled to break free. She did not speak to him but he learned her name from the crying pleas of the children.

Preacher often visited and inspected the wound and said his new name with a smile before leaving. Able to prop his back against the warm plaster, he sat and ate stale bread with mash and watched the children in the yard. The soft sunlight spread across his legs and warmed his skin. In certain light, the scar on his knee cast a shadow.

Two boys intrigued by him snuck to the window and watched him with only eyes shown but when he rattled off in Akara, they scattered like birds.

The wound ached but he found himself able to stand and maneuver his shuffled steps from wall to wall. A pair of shorts covered him and the cumbersome fabric felt weighty on his legs and he wondered how the whites could wear such uncomfortable clothes. The thick book sat at one end and he stared at the cover before turning back and pacing away.

He had just resumed his spot by the window and placed his head against the wall when she entered. A steaming bowl cupped in her hand. Though she tried, she still glanced up and his eyes caught hers.

Where have you been? he asked as he straightened his back on the wall.

I have been busy.

She hit the spoon three times on the side of the bowl.

I was wondering when you would come. The other woman scares me.

She brought the bowl over. Another dress, pocked with sunflowers, draped down her body. The sunlight stretched past his legs and caught her at the waist by his bedside.

She sighed and extended her hands and he took the bowl.

Her brothers were killed by Akara tribesmen when she was a girl.

He looked down at the bowl. A faint guilt turned his lips down and he spooned the sweet mash into his mouth with a slurp. Rebecca brushed her hands down the front of her dress. Only the sound of his food lingered a moment.

How is your wound? she asked.

Better.

Her teeth gripped her bottom lip a moment before she adjusted items on the medicine table. He watched her as he ate.

How did you come here? he asked.

She did not look at him.

You said you are mingi. How did you survive?

She paused.

Preacher told me I was very young. My mother had been with a man. But they had not taken their vows. The Elders did not want a mingi to curse their crops or cattle. She knew my fate before I was even born. Preacher had built this orphanage for children like me. Forgotten children. Cursed. Somehow, my mother had heard from a Mujar woman about a white man who wanted mingi and walked a long way to meet him. She could not tell anyone. Not even my father. They all think I am at the bottom of the Omo. When the day came for me to enter this world, she gave birth to me in the bush and handed me to Preacher in the night.

The discordant words left her lips and seemed to drop to the floor pulled from the air by the weight of a painful origin. A vision of her as a proud Akara woman came to him wearing countless bronze bracelets wrapped around her wrists and neck. Yet the vision drowned in red. He said nothing.

She seemed to return from somewhere. "

That is how I came to be here.

Are you happy? he asked. His guts boiled with tension more than when they circled the Kangatum camp.

She turned her somber eyes toward him. Those eyes he feared and desired to swim inside their depths.

If God granted me the choice to either go back to that night, if I were not as I am but an acceptable child for my people, if my life as an Akara became all that life could have dreamed for me, I would still be that babe in Preacher's arms.

The spoon remained clutched in his hand as the mash dripped onto his thumb. His throat filled with the words of his life, piled and scrambling to snatch up his tongue but he swallowed hard so the bulge in his neck bobbed. The clamor so violent, he choked on them and coughed. He did not know whether the words fought his body or his body fought the words.

She had kept her eyes on him and they pierced his skin and bones with more fire than the bullets at the river. Her silence caught him aflame and higher and higher the words stung his throat and the ends of the letters scratched the back of his tongue. It caught him and a sound squeaked from his lips and he slapped his palm against his mouth, eyes wide.

She whispered, Tell me.

He choked again. Perhaps, he wondered, taking life was easier than giving it. Perhaps the act of taking life absolves one of the ache of its consequence. To impose on another the discord within one's own heart gifts a reprieve of the exactitudes of emotion. However, in the end, the reprieve is only a stay of confusion until the words stack and pile until a body can no longer contain them.

Her eyes swallowed him and down he sank into their depths and, though the recognition of how to breathe terrified him, he opened his mouth.

I am cursed. The useless son. The brother who survived and who brings shame on his family. The one who escaped the Valley and the river. I am the lost boy. The one who fails. The drifter who belongs to no tribe or no god. Nothing. The coward who pierces the heart of the old man who saved him. A rogue in the wilderness. The spiller of blood. The one who stalks the land and pursues tribes like a lion. No, a jackal. The one who kills to kill. The soulless warrior. The portrait of the damned. This is who I am and, even as this Moses, I will still be Tesfahun. I will still be Gägäma. I will still be Däm Afasash. Though these will be my names, I will always be mingi.

In one breath, it escaped from him and he inhaled after the last word as if coming to the surface to breathe.

Rebecca's eyes pooled as his lungs pressed into his chest and they devoured him in a manner terrifying and heartening. The taste of the names he had never spoken left a bitter residue on his lips and scraped against his tongue. The pools on her eyelids caught the remnants of sunlight before the sun slept behind the mountains to the west.

You are Moses now, she said.

She stepped closer until he could smell the sweat from her skin and the powder of flour. Her once averted eyes now focused on his and her hand raised, finger slightly limp, and brushed the tear sliding down his cheek. A single tear he did not know escaped. Who did he cry for? Perhaps for himself. For the old man. For Wagaye. Even Mamo. Maybe he cried for her who now took his hand and her soft palm slid atop his slit knuckles and the blood they held.

The last vestige of the red sun lingered as if hesitant to descend. Its captive glare dropped behind the mountain top and light faded from all creation.

Rebecca's head bowed and she whispered in solemn voice a chant in a language he did not know. A language not of Akara, or Muhar or Kangatum or even city folk but of foreign tongues.

The unknown words settled in his chest, through bone and blood, and nestled their way into his beating heart.

He wondered if this one god had broken down the blood-thirsty demons that inhabited his body and replaced their presence with its own. Or had this new god killed them.

He hung on to her strange words and tears flowed again but he let them fall from the faint stubble of his chin. Her nails dug into his knuckles but he did not care.

If she carried this one god with her, he must exist.

XLI

His remainder of the time spent recovering, Rebecca visited him each day bearing soup, bread, or conversation.

The pain lessened and he accepted the dull ache around the opening as a necessary part of his time under this new roof. Martha, scowling and harried, still came and restocked the medical supplies without a word. The children still played their game at his window and he, in return, spooked them with a shout and they ran in terrified ecstasy from him. The crowd of children grew until he found no time to rest, embroiled in games with boys and girls unaware of their clefts or shriveled hands. A family of misfits.

When the children returned to their classrooms, he either slept or held Preacher's leather book in his lap and turned the delicate pages. The whisper of the paper rubbed against one another. The sound may have spoken actual words or perhaps not. The ink formed in incoherent clusters before his eyes but he followed their shape as if each curve were a path toward this one god of Rebecca's. A path he could not follow. He recalled how Preacher had told him about this god and he searched among the gibberish of its pages.

When the voices returned outside, he placed the heavy book on his lap and watched as they poured into the yard. Limitless futures resonated among them and, in each face, lay the remnants of their curse. Present but faded like a wound about to scar.

The distant cliffs and the Omo, always loomed in the distance behind their jovial faces.

Two boys snuck to the window and jumped out, startling Moses, and he slapped at their hands tight around the sill and they skipped off with laughter in their wake. He turned back to the entrance and saw Preacher, arms folded, smiling.

"They like you", he said.

Moses shrugged.

He sidled next to the cot. "How are you feel?"

Moses paused. Why do you take these mingi children?

Preacher scratched under his rough chin as he looked out the window at two girls jumping rope.

"You Akara? I could ask the question to you."

The Akara believe they are cursed. That the gods and spirits have shown disfavor with them and will curse the people, their lands, and their cattle. They have to sacrifice for the tribe.

"Why do you say 'they'?"

Moses stared with his head cocked to the side, silent.

"You Akara but you speak like you are not Akara."

Tell me about this book, he said, jamming his dirty fingernail into the cover at his bedside.

Preacher's eyes followed to the black book. His eyes pondering with a vacant glaze. Moses stared back, examining the features of Preacher's face.

"What about it?"

Moses placed his palm on the cover.

I look at this book each day. I cannot read the words but there is something about them that makes me feel like they were written for me. I need to know what it says.

Preacher's eyes drifted to the book then lifted back to Moses. He tucked his buttoned shirt down his shorts and Moses believed he saw the thoughts grinding behind Preacher's eyes that made the pupils tremble.

"In a way, we have all wrote book."

So you wrote it?

Preacher sat on the edge of the cot with his back to the window. He clasped his hands as he leaned forward and the sound of children carried through the window. He reached out and took the book from Moses' beside and held the thick sides with both hands. The weight visible in his palms.

"Many men wrote this book over long time. They stories of life. About family and God and truth. About kings and slaves. Distant lands. Smart words about love and anger and murder. This book life. There are death but life are first. It talk of men who fought and died for God."

Moses ears piqued. The foreign words unwound their fixed shape and transformed into image after image. Kings and weapons collided in battle constructed from the only images retained in his memory. Primal constructs that resembled his father's silhouette.

I want no part of a book of death.

Preacher smiled. "Moses, this is book of life."

Moses paused with a querulous expression fixed on his face.

"It also talk of one man. Important man. He die for all people because he love all people. His name are Jesus."

He sat slack jawed at the strange tale.

Why did he die? he asked Preacher.

Preacher turned to his right and his blue eyes shone toward him. "Would you die for Kangatum man?"

Moses shook his head. I would never die for such cockroaches.

Mamo's words in his mouth paralyzed him. The taste of the sounds a bitter residue.

"It is violent mystery one would give life to save his enemy. God sacrifice his only son for all of us. For ones who kill him. Mock him. For you and me. That is sacrifice."

The clear words sunk deep in his chest. He wondered how this god could kill his own son for the sake of man. And how such a son would be willing to give his life for the sake of those who wronged him. This perverted justice circled his skull and with each revolution, the gravity of such a sacrifice nagged at the consciousness of his very being.

Why would your god do such a thing to his own son? He sounds like an Akara.

Preacher even smiled. "For love. Not fear."

Moses dropped his eyes and rested his gaze on the book in which this legend resided. He knew he could believe in such a hero. In such a god. But perhaps he would not.

I want to hear these stories. Can you tell them to me?

Preacher bounced the book in his hands. "You will. When you are ready, you will be at school. I will teach."

He smiled then tossed the book onto Moses' lap. The surprising weight startled him and he lurched forward. His hands clutched the leather sides.

Preacher leaned toward Moses and landed two quick pats atop his thigh before standing. He stretched his arms wide then proceeded to the medicine table and placed vials, bandages and other items on a wooden tray, whistling. Moses watched him gather his items and then lift the tray in a casual manner. Before he passed the doorframe, Preacher glanced back and winked. His whistle growing faint after his departure.

He rubbed his hands on the leather cover. At times, it felt coarse and others smooth. He thought on this god who would sacrifice his son for his enemy and if he could do such a thing if he had a son. He knew his father could.

His fingers dipped into the engraved tree on the cover and, though he did not know this god nor his son, he knew within his bones that that god would not send children to rivers and valleys. He would not send Dawit to retrieve the blood of his brother's killer.

Perhaps this god was mingi as well.

XLII

With the reluctance of Martha, she allowed him to leave the hut and walk among the buildings of the orphanage. Rebecca, her head wrap pulled tight and another floral dress that swooped at her steps, gave him the tour.

They walked along the dusty, worn path to the building he saw outside his window and the warmth of the sun on his skin rekindled the reality he was still alive. The same grey-toned plaster walls surrounded the structure but, inside, cracks zigged across the cold, hard floor under long wooden tables and chairs facing a black wall. Smeared and dust-white with words and letters he did not understand written across the face.

Moses walked to the wall and swiped his hand down and left four black lines in the white dust. The ends of his fingers dusted like Kangatum warriors. He examined his fingers and looked to Rebecca who giggled behind her hand.

This is where the smaller children are taught. They sit in these chairs and the teacher helps them learn to read and write and to do math problems. This is where I received my education, she said. Her nostalgic eyes canvassed the room and the small faces intent at their schoolwork.

Moses wiped his hand on his shirt. What is math?

She laughed and gestured for him to follow. Another building, smaller but of the same condition, stood on the other side of where he healed.

The older children, teenagers, learn in this room. This is where I teach sometimes.

Do they learn from Preacher's book? he asked.

Everyone does.

Will you teach me?

She ran her hand along one of the tables, nicked and scarred and marked. He saw two rectangular boxes imbued with a greyish film in the fibers. His curious hands picked them off the teacher's desk and slammed the two together. A white cloud burst in front of him and hung like a mist before the particles fell to reveal his dark face now an ashen white.

Rebecca's laugh echoed against the plaster walls and tin roof. He spit and then, unable to think of another reaction, laughed with her.

They walked in the waning morning to a narrow building. The common grey plaster replaced by an earthy red that reminded him of the banks of the Omo. A tree he had seen only on Preacher's book hung by the door. Rebecca walked just behind him and he stopped at the door to touch the wood of the tree. Smooth and gentle, he had never felt wanza or bedena that resembled such wood.

This is an odd tree.

Rebecca stopped, looked from the tree to Moses.

This is the cross.

I saw it on Preacher's book.

This is the Cross of Calvary where Jesus Christ was crucified. They nailed his hands and his feet until he died.

She said this, pointing to the outermost distances of the cross where those hands and feet once stuck.

His brow bunched. On this tree? he asked.

She chuckled to herself.

No. Not *this* tree.

Though she laughed at his ignorance, the tone of her voice made such details trivial. Moses leaned on the wood and felt his body pressed into the rigidity of its essence so he did not need to use his own weight to stay upright.

You say this Jesus was the son of your god yet he sent him to this tree to die.

She nodded.

So this Jesus was mingi.

He died to save mingi.

He paused and stared at the cross. Why would a father do that to his son?

She adjusted the head wrap that loosened around her temples.

Love.

Only thoughts of Kelile came to him. Only minutes had determined if he was the one sacrificed and he did not doubt his father would sacrifice him. He doubted for such a noble cause as this Jesus. Kelile's hands already bore the blood of one son.

Rebecca placed a gentle hand and nudged him from the cross and through the doorway.

The room smelled of flora and candles burned in metal tins lined along a small riser where another, larger cross suspended on the wall. Benches lined like crops of sorghum stretched toward the back wall and, spaced on the seats, sat orange books. Miniature versions of Preacher's.

He wandered between the rows and walked an absent maze he knew not led him to the pulpit. At the riser, he stepped onto the shaky platform among the host of burning candles. Perfumed fragrance overwhelmed him in the shadow of the cross and he ran his fingers over the black and white keys and the strange sound startled him.

Rebecca giggled as if amused at a child's first encounter.

That is a piano.

What is it for?

To sing songs to Jesus.

He inched forward and pressed the ebony key and the tone moaned from the mystic box. His finger rested on the it until the sound faded. Motionless, he stood entranced by the novelty of the notes.

Rebecca came to his side and, placing her hands next to his, she pressed the keys into harmonies. His ears rang and the vibrations rattled his soul and he longed for more. Smooth fingers danced atop the keys in sequences. A divine foreign sound filled his spirit.

He paused, finger still on the ebony, and watched how graceful her dark hands moved against the white. Then the unknown song needed no words. Only her hands.

When she finished, they walked outside. A warm breeze brushed against their faces and it carried laughter. The children played outside the house filled with bunk beds and cots. More bodies than beds. The two boys who engaged Moses in games ran up to him, mouths full of flatbread.

Are you orphans like us? one boy, whose malformed palette allowed mashed bread to expose itself.

He looked down at the playful boys.

Not exactly, he replied.

With a shrug, the two ran off to and chased the checkered ball like rabid hounds. Preacher emerged from behind a shed carrying a shovel.

"Ah, you are walking. Good, good. I see Rebecca are showing you the place."

He nodded and Rebecca's coy demeanor overtook her eyes.

Preacher stood the shovel spade first into the ground at his feet. A young girl waved and Preacher pat her head as she walked past. Books tucked under her arm.

"Looks like you will be learning soon?" he asked in his bad Akara. "Perhaps I teach you English so I no sound so ill."

The two suppressed their laughter but Preacher erupted in a loud guffaw enough to inspire unaware children to join for the sake of laughing.

Preacher lifted the shovel and gestured toward a teenage boy to follow him, speaking in his language. As he passed, Preacher placed a hand on Moses's shoulder and nodded at Rebecca before passing in his long-legged gait between buildings with the boy close behind.

The small children swirled around them in a frenzy of youth. Rebecca at his side, he breathed a long breath into his lungs and a vision of the bones of the Valley rose up in his eyes and they danced also and ran from their unmarked graves in shrill leaps of freedom. The clatter of their bones, stripped of flesh and blood and muscle but propelled by spirit. Perhaps his nameless brother ran with them. The wind brushed against his smooth skull, between the gaps in bones. A strong desire to run with him leapt inside Moses as he stood between the dead and the living.

The children walked single file toward the building bearing the cross and Moses, heads above, followed. Martha led them then stood at the door and pushed each in the small of their backs to fill in the benches. Her mannish hands made Moses lung forward and bump the girl in front of him as he passed.

He sat among the children who whispered and fidgeted until small bodies filled the benches. The children behind him leaned from side to side and commented on how they could not see Preacher because of the new orphan. Moses slouched with no success and leaned forward to move until he heard the piano's banging keys echo through the building. He looked to the stage but saw Martha sitting at the piano, pounding the keys with such force he wondered if the instrument had killed her sister.

The high voices sang around him. Every mouth knew the words and some of the younger ones danced jittery steps to the swaying melody. They spoke in Preacher's tongue and the only 'Jesus' and 'blood' made sense to him.

He swiveled his head around, spying every face and every hand clap. Preacher stood near the piano with his book open in his hands and his eyes closed. Moses stood witness to a ceremony beyond any he had encountered or could imagine. The chaos of the fire and the chants of his childhood had disappeared and by this Jesus who died for his enemies. He wondered if this Jesus would kill the spirits of the Omo should they ever engage in battle.

The song died and Preacher walked to the front of the riser and bowed his head to the floor. With eyes closed, he prayed and the children, in a chorus of lamentations, uttered the same words. Their repentant faces all to their feet and hands clasped at their waist. And then, silence.

Without warning, they all sat together and Moses, head bowed, remained standing as giggles fluttered around him. He opened his eyes and sat down and stared into his lap.

Across his knee, he saw the long scar and he felt the suffocating collapse of the river and then the face of the old man stood above him. Then it passed and Preacher stood at the front and began to speak in the same language of the song and of the prayer.

No translation was afforded him but he sat rapt with his eyes wandering from Preacher to Martha, to the faces of the congregation. The massive cross behind Preacher towered above him.

The boy and girl on either side of him fidgeted with the edges of their shirts and skirts. The boy rocked on his haunches and Moses sensed the stare of the little boy.

Drifting among a sea of youth, his soul settled with a peace inside him. The unfamiliar world he now inhabited held more security and comfort than he had ever known as an Akara boy. As if the bodies within the walls barred the destruction of reality where no hands could drown him nor blades or bullets could pierce. The white man who stood above him, book open and reading from its pages, brought no weapons or flashes or dammed rivers like the whispers of the tribes.

Time crept on but he did not notice for Martha had risen and returned to the piano and he wished Rebecca's hands were placed on the keys instead. Preacher finished and said a prayer among bowed heads and the noises pounded from the piano and they sang to Jesus and god and blood and other mysteries.

When the song had finished, Preacher dismissed the children and they rose to exit as they entered. At the door, Preacher loitered, hands clutching the book with his black-filled nails, and greeted each in turn with slapping hands and quick rubs of the scalp. When Moses arrived before him, he did not realize the tear tracks on his cheek and wondered if Jesus had powers to cause others to cry for no reason. Preacher smiled and placed a firm hand on Moses's shoulder.

Moses smiled. Will you teach me to read this book?

Preacher nodded with a smile as if he expected the question and a tender hand ushered him out the door and into the day.

XLIII

Clouds sprinkled rain and clattered on the tin roofs like the chorus of a thousand stones.

The noise rose to such extremes, Rebecca sat silent across from Moses and waited until the rains lessened so they could hear each other when they spoke. He noticed her habits and how she restrained her anger by pinching the skin at her elbow between her nails or how she covered her mouth when she laughed. When Preacher had instructed her to tutor Moses, he thought maybe this god did hear one's thoughts and desires. She told him he was a child of god. But he knew his father and he was not a god.

He spent his mornings with her learning the language of Preacher. She told him they called it English and he hated the duplicity of such a language. Words of dual meaning yet held no similar sounds yet sounds, thought the same, held different meanings. Two sounds for one letter and the odd shapes in which they were formed, and he wondered how a language could be formed from such strange symbols.

After the first lesson, he hurled a wooden chair that splintered and left a gouge in the plaster walls. But Rebecca's quiet eyes stabbed him with regret and, later that evening, he found some wanza and worked through the light of the oil lamps to repair the damage he had done.

In the afternoons, he sat at a small desk among other children to hear Martha's lessons. She instructed in Akara, Muhar, and Kangatum and, often times, lapsed into English where her words seldom made their way to his understanding.

With dusty smears across her black dress, Martha wrote numbers on the chalk boards and children raised their hands to be called upon as Moses watched, feeling one step behind the others. When they had finished the number lessons, they ran into the daylight and played Mamba with the younger children and an older boy named Isaiah taught him the game of football. He showed him how to stop his hands from touching the ball and how to kick with the inside of his foot, not the toe.

Two Muhar girls with cleft palates swung a rope as he tried to jump through but the slack rope slapped against his face. No stick fighters or ceremonies. No blood. Only games.

They returned to the classroom and each child opened a book like Preacher's, which he learned they called a Bible.

These were the words of god, Martha said.

They read stories about kings and the creation of man and about giants who roamed the earth to be defeated by children. Of rain that poured for days and killed all life and of fire from the sky. Hearing the stories each day, the reality of blood seeped deeper into his heart. He wondered how a god would ask his own people to destroy another race or how he allowed them such power as to topple walls with only their voices. The more he learned about this god, he was convinced he was Akara.

A week passed and he sat by the fire after the children slept in their bunks. Outside the buildings, he could hear the faint calls of jackals but distant as if they knew the sanctity of this place. Rebecca and Preacher joined him, seated in wooden chairs around the fire. Martha absent of her own volition. Above them a canopy of stars.

Moses rubbed his hands in front of the flame and warmed on his hands.

This place is like the heaven in your book, Moses said.

Rebecca smiled.

Preacher chuckled. "At least in heaven, they have run water."

The joke passed without a response as Preacher settled onto his seat. The fire glow cast across his bearded face. He looked at Moses.

"So this place is heaven to you?" Preacher asked.

Yes, yes, it is.

"I no say I agree. But I glad you is happy."

A slight pause.

Can I ask you something?

"Go."

You say your god is full of love. But his book says so many things about death and murder. God says these things. When I hear them, they make me think of where I am from. How can that be?

Preacher leaned back and placed his hands behind his head. The lanky elbows jutted from the side of his head and he lifted his chin toward the stars before turning to Rebecca.

"Can you answer?" he asked.

Rebecca gave an uncertain glance as if questioning him without words.

Preacher nodded and she took a deep breath and then looked Moses.

Every man has the capability to kill. It is what has been in us from birth since the Fall. God knows this. But, he has also given us a choice. To kill or not to kill. The god you hear about doesn't desire blood. He desires sacrifice. It is not his will for violence. That is why he gave up his son to be crucified. To satisfy our quest for blood in order that we might be saved. Blood is the only thing that can save us. It was blood that Cain spilled that made this thirst and it is in the blood of Christ that the thirst can be satisfied.

Moses recoiled back when he heard the name. Rebecca startled back.

"What is it?" Preacher asked.

I cannot hear that name.

"Cain?"

He shook his head as if fighting back tears.

The Akara believe taking the life of one's brother is a crime no one can forgive. If I were god, I would have killed that man.

"That is why we are not God."

Moses reached down at his side and lifted the black book and flipped through the pages and pointed at a random spot.

This book talks about a man named David. He was a king. And in all these pages, he is at war. He and his men kill and spill blood wherever they go. And your god tells him to do it and helps them. He helps them to kill their enemies. How can Jesus like this when he tells you to be kind and to love?

Rebecca lifted her eyes from stoking the fire in absent pokes.

Moses continued. God must be Akara.

Preacher leaned forward, his pale face lit with flame and his eyes reflected the dance before him. Rebecca looked up and leaned forward as she spoke.

Violence is the only language our people speak. Even after Babel, it remained as the only understanding between men. I cannot try to understand the ways of God. But I will have faith. And if violence is the only way for God to speak with us, for us to come close and feel his presence in our lives, then I will endure that violence for the remainder of my days.

Moses and Rebecca's eyes met as Preacher spoke.

He sat across from the two, book open and the breath of life seemed to blow in his face. He held the mystery in his hands and, though he did not understand the words just yet, he found comfort in their presence.

The fire whispered and its embers burst with a crack and shot a splash of sparks into the night sky. Preacher procured a knife, not a crude Akara blade, but one of shiny metal and an inlaid handle, and whittled at a long, knotty branch and flipped shavings into the fire that the flames consumed before they even hit the ash.

Moses watched his methodical hands and he found himself sitting next to Mamo and watching Teferi in the circle of blood-lusters. His eyes appeared lidless, unblinking, and Preacher caught a glimpse of Moses vacant face when he lifted the end of the sharp stick to his face.

"What troubles you, Moses?"

Memory snapped off and he saw their faces as if for the first time. The residue of those days still lingered in his gut. The briefest of thoughts came and left, wondering if memory could find a way to nestle and burrow into bones and never leave or if it somehow subverted scars and found eternal residence in our corporeal bodies. These thoughts troubled him and, when he spoke to dismiss them, they snuck from his bones and into his tongue.

I was never a good Akara boy. I could see it in the eyes of my father and mother. Sometimes they looked at me and I knew they wished my brother had been born first. That it were my bones in the Valley. And sometimes, I wished he had too. Even when I gave in and my blades drank for the first time, I knew I only acted. Like some spirit hidden within me had used me like a puppet. Some part of me longed for something. Some mystery I could not find or understand. My anger took me away from my people, my family. Took me farther than I ever thought I would go. There was a time when I believed I might wear the ostrich feather or hang the lion skin in my doorway. But I know that will not be. Not on my own. And now you find me. You healed me. Taught me the way in which I should go. You teach me about your god and Jesus who dies for his enemies. He could have killed them as we do, but he let them kill him. How can that be? How can a man possess so much love he would die to save his enemies? I wonder if he truly was a man because a man does not thirst for his own blood. Tell me, Preacher, can this Jesus take away the blood from my hands?

Noise from the surrounding dark chattered in the distance. Preacher's hunched body, weight forward on his knees, held his palms to the fire and looked at Rebecca. Perhaps for guidance or out of thought.

In the firelight, the shadows pulled at his face and lengthened the contours of his features. Moses waited, the heat from the fire rivaling the one inside. Rebecca's head hung but her eyes rolled upward, her furtive gaze watching.

"Yes, he can."

The words hovered over the crackling fire as if snatched by the flames to burn with more heat, more fire. Moses watched the flames a moment and the embers that rose like fireflies into the air and he followed one speck until it reached high enough it disappeared among the stars above. He leaned his head back and gazed into the night at the endless range of lights above him and toward a god who may or may not reside within the darkness. The luminescent specks coalesced above him and took on faces of the past with solemn contentment at the one who witnessed them. And, perhaps, among those faces of his past, nestled between the dead and the living, the eyes, the nose, the mouth of a man never seen before yet his presence imparted comfort and peace of time, ancient and immemorial. A man who reigned by spilling no other blood but his own.

The others watched Moses as tears he often fought now flowed freely down his cheeks and pocked the dirt at his feet. Preacher stood and walked round the fire and sat beside Moses, eyes still heavenward. Moses did not look to him but only to the face above and spoke in sobs.

I want to know this man.

XLIV

The red waters of the Omo snaked through the region.

From above, his eyes scanned the land of his birth and the huts could be seen in the distance. Too far to recognize but focused enough to know his home lay forward. Yes, his home.

Children splashed in the same water at the same edge where Dawit swam. New boys jammed sticks and dropped sorghum seeds into the mud. Rebecca squeezed his hand and he turned his misty eyes toward hers and she lifted her body on her toes and kissed his lips so softly he could have mistaken it for a breeze. In his other hand, the book of life nestled into his palm.

He looked once again on the land and felt the presence of his scars. The wounds still felt but the new skin strong. Planting his feet in the present and the mystery of where his steps may lead. She looked down on the valley with him.

It is different than I imagined, she said.

What did you expect?

The breeze from the waters whispered across her face.

I don't know.

The smoke from fire pits coiled upward into the blue sky among the small huts.

These are our people, Rebecca.

She gripped his hand in both of hers. The dress hanging round her ankles danced in the wind and the swaying grass.

Is this home? she asked with her fingers wrapped in his.

He slipped his fingers from hers and placed a gentle hand on her belly.

Where we belong.

Her worried smile faded and she placed her forehead on his. They lingered on the threshold for some time before Moses exhaled his ghosts of memory. He had long been far removed from this land and the fear his people may reject him lingered in his spirit.

But he gripped the book and the hand of his bride and knew what lay ahead was of no consequence. His body now belonged to the one who had saved him.

They descended the hill and walked along the river, past the sorghum fields and the trail he used to run down. Past old women with clay pots balanced on their heads. Naked children chasing each other. The smoke, the huts, the people closer and closer under the sun. They said nothing as they drew close, even as they entered the village and walked between huts, past Bale's and the others. The hut of the crying mother. The land stationary, a monument as if he never left. Every stick, every stone, every speck of dust placed as if by his memory. By the flawless remembering of time.

And it brought him before the hut at the edge of the village. The savannah and tall grass with stations of wanza trees behind.

He and Rebecca stopped far from the home. The now tattered lion skin hung dirtied by the land and the hands that moved it. A silence permeated the clearing and doubt crept into him. They looked at each other and his heart pounded in his chest and blasts of scenarios fired through his mind. And in the chaos of his body, he saw the lion move.

Those mournful eyes peeked from the doorway and lingered in the shadows of that room.

They paralyzed him and he waited, gripping Rebecca's hand so tight she fought back the urge to cry out. A recognition came over those sad eyes and they floated from the dark into the light until he saw her frail body in the day. She did not blink. Her eyes deciding if they had seen a ghost.

Then she called to the hut.

A man emerged. His beard and hair now sprinkled with white and his deep-set features even further so. The same features he would one day display. The old couple stood a step from their doorway.

Moses took two steps forward. Their eyes and stoic features watched him, waiting, and he returned with his own bewildered gaze. The ostrich feather tattered but risen high, fluttering in the breeze under the darkening sky. Nearly as dark as his mother's stained eyes.

When he looked back, Rebecca stood where he had left, clutching the Bible to her chest with one hand on her swollen belly. He looked from the hut to his bride and back again in silence.

His buttoned shirt and long trousers suffocated him as if he burned on the inside. He glanced back to his mother and father and then grabbed at the buttons. Yanking and pulling until the clothes Preacher had given him lay in a heap at his feet in the dust and he stood naked in the land of his youth.

Moses, what are you doing? Rebecca called out with a hand on her expectant belly.

He stared at his parents in the doorway of his home and the faces of Dawit and Dunga and the Old Man and Demissie and Preacher and Jesus all those who had walked him to this moment seemed to arise from the land and surround the hut.

Moses! She called once more.

With a sigh, he turned toward her, feeling the cool breeze on his naked skin. His eyes set.

Call me Tesfahun.

Author's Note

The novel you just read is based on a true story. In fact, it is based on the true stories of many children who disappeared in the river and the bush. While the tribes and characters are fictionalized, there is far more fact than fiction in *The Cry of Dry Bones*.

Among the tribes of the Omo Valley, mingi killings are a common practice stemming from the belief these children, due to their physical deformities or circumstance, are cursed and will bring pestilence, drought, famine or war on the tribe. Most of these children are thrown in the river or left in the wilderness at only a few months old.

I first heard about this practice at church. Through some connections, a family in our congregation had adopted a mingi girl from the Karo tribe. Until then, the term meant nothing until a non-profit called Drawn From Water spoke during the service and detailed their work in the Omo Valley. Night raids to intercept a child before they were murdered, convincing the tribal elders to allow them to keep the child, and housing and feeding rescued mingi children were all part of their operation. I was captivated.

Over time, a novel emerged from this idea and shaped into what you read today after many revisions spanning several years. The most important aspect of this process was being true to the people of the Omo and their practices, presenting this facsimile of their culture and beliefs, not as monsters, but as humans navigating a complex and challenging world.

Tesfahun's journey embodies this complexity and the importance of finding one's own path regardless of where their origins exist. Hopefully, the beauty of the Akara, an amalgamation of various Omo tribes, is a representation of the Omotic people.

Drawn from Water, some photographers, and iterations of OmoChild, non-profits who spread knowledge and rescued 'cursed' children, have had success in convincing several tribes to abolish the killing of mingi children. However, some tribes still continue the belief, however, it is a challenge to undue centuries of tradition.

If you are interested in learning more, I suggest the documentary *Omo Child: The River and the Bush* which follows Lale Labuko, a Karo man whose older sisters were mingi, tries to end the mingi tradition.

Acknowledgements

First, I need to thank my wife who always reads my manuscripts and tells me the truth and encourages me through the emotional roller coaster of writing.

I would also like to thank Joseph Scapellato for his help in fixing the pacing issues in the original draft.

A thank you goes out to Stevan at Adelaide Books for giving the story its first introduction into the world.

Thanks to the writers and readers who have contributed reviews to this story.

Thank you to National Geographic, *Omo Child: The River and the Bush*, OmoChild.org, and the other sources that provided crucial research and insight into the tribes, topography, wildlife and culture of the Omo region.

Much gratitude goes out to all the tireless workers who seek to save mingi children from the river and the bush. You are the unsung heroes and I hope this story brings all of your good deeds into the light.

A final thank you goes out to the writers, filmmakers and musicians that inspired me during the process of writing this book.

To stay up to date on events, new releases and new writings
about N.T. McQueen, visit or follow at:

www.ntmcqueen.com
Twitter (@NTMAuthor),
Instagram (@ntmcqueen)
Facebook.

Also by N.T. McQueen

Between Lions and Lambs: a novel

Everyone has a past including Ezekiel Clemens, the world's most
influential and noticeable evangelist. Despite traveling the globe
preaching and speaking to hundreds of thousands of followers,
this man of God is haunted. At his side is Gerald, a friend and
accomplice in hiding Ezekiel's sinful secrets.

On the day of one of their televised meetings, faces from their
previous lives return and force the two to confront the demons
they have tried to so hard to run from.